MW01265347

She had a new job with a superstar actor and a new roommate, so all her troubles should be over, shouldn't they?

Twenty minutes later, the pizza guy buzzed them to let him know he was there.

"I'll grab it. Be back in a flash," Hudson said.

When he left, Sonny smiled at her good fortune. He was not a creep at all, and this set up would really benefit her financially. She needed to remind herself to thank Vivian for the recommendation.

When Hudson came back up with the pizza, he was wary and had a strange look on his face.

"What's wrong? Did they get the order wrong?"

"Uh, no," he said and showed her what was in his hand. "I think these are for you."

It was a bouquet of dead, wilted flowers with a ribbon intertwined around the dried up petals and baby's breath. On it read her name, *Sonny Winslow*. It was the kind of arrangement you would see at a funeral home.

With trembling hands, she reached for the card, and it read:

Any friends of Parker Maxwell is not a friend of mine.

I pick them off one by one like dead decaying flowers on a vine.

“What the hell? Who is Parker Maxwell?” Hudson asked.

“It’s Daxton Knight’s new character for his upcoming movie.”

Actor Daxton Knight is a rising star and appears to be have everything, including fame, fortune, and his pick of gorgeous women, but appearances can be deceiving as he begins to receive some distasteful hate mail. It seems someone holds a grudge against the superstar, and when Dax relocates to film his next movie, he is assigned a temporary personal assistant. Sonny Winslow is an aspiring writer looking to get her book published, but she needs to make some money in the meantime. She and Dax get off to a rather rough start when his model girlfriend takes an instant dislike to the author, and Dax insinuates Sonny is using his fame to help her career. But when Sonny starts receiving the same threatening messages, she and Dax join forces to figure out who their stalker could be. To their dismay, the danger mounts with each encounter from their unknown predator, and they must watch each other's back while still working together on the film. Each scene intensifies, and you aren't sure how it will end until the director yells, "That's a Wrap."

KUDOS for *That's a Wrap*

In *That's a Wrap* by J D Davis, Sonny Winslow needs a job. A friend recommends her to an actor's agent, and Sonny is hired as the actor's personal assistant. The actor, Daxton Knight, is a hunk that women can't seem to resist, but Sonny just wants to do her job and go home to write. She's a budding author waiting for a book deal and just needs to pay the bills in the meantime. But when Dax starts getting hate mail that mentions Sonny, the two put flirtations aside to find out who is stalking them. Is it an old girlfriend who had her heart broken, Dax's current ex-lover who's insanely jealous of Sonny, or could it be someone from Dax's mysterious past? The story is moving, exciting, and tense. Filled with wonderful characters, fast-paced action, and plenty of suspense, it will keep you on the edge of your seat all the way through. ~ *Taylor Jones, The Review Team of Taylor Jones & Regan Murphy*

That's a Wrap by JD Davis is the story of a struggling new author, trying to pay the bills until she can sell her novel, and an actor with a mysterious past that has come back to haunt him. Sonny Winslow has written a novel and now she is trying to sell it, but until she does, she needs to find a way to pay her bills. When she is offered a well-paying job as the assistant to superstar actor, Daxton Knight, who's in town to film his new movie, it seems too good to be true. And like most things that seem that way, it is. Daxton is arrogant, self-centered, disorganized, and he has a super model girlfriend who is extremely jealous of Sonny. It makes for very tense working conditions. But things only get worse when Sonny starts to get hate mail due to her association with Dax. As they compare notes, Dax confesses that he has also been getting hate mail that started just before he came to town, and he has no idea who the deranged stalker is. As the threats become more serious, Sonny and Dax begin to fear for their lives, especially when things start happening to those they love. *That's a Wrap* combines mystery, suspense, and romance for a chilling and poignant tale of two innocent people harassed by a psycho with a grudge. It's one that will keep you up turning pages from beginning to end. ~ *Regan Murphy, The Review Team of Taylor Jones & Regan Murphy*

ACKNOWLEDGMENTS

A huge thank you goes out to my family and friends for allowing me to take little pieces of our real life to help me develop loveable quirky characters to take part in an enjoyable-to-write fictitious story. As always, thank you to my readers for all of your support.

THAT'S A WRAP

JD Davis

A Black Opal Books Publication

GENRE: MYSTERY-DETECTIVE/CRIME THRILLER

THAT'S A WRAP

Cover Design by Jackson Cover Design

Print ISBN: 978-1-626949-79-9

First Publication: AUGUST 2018

Published by Black Opal Books **http://www.blackopalbooks.com**

DEDICATION

To my husband, thank you for encouraging me to pursue my passion and challenging me to go beyond my comfort zone to push myself to the next level.

To TMZ: You are my reason for living and are proof that dreams can come true. It still stands true—if you can dream it, you can achieve it. Always be kind, never stop reaching, trust your instincts, listen to the voice within. It is more than your conscience, it is God directing you, and always believe in yourself as much as I believe in you.
~ Love always, Mom

PROLOGUE

The air was thick, and he could barely breathe. Sweat dripped down his brow, stinging his eyes. He rubbed them to clear his vision, but it was to no avail. His mouth was full of dust, and he inhaled the scent of gunpowder. The sound of shots being fired filled his ears, and he looked around to find the rest of his squadron.

His heart raced at the thought of poking his head up from behind the barricade where he had taken cover. Part of him wanted to stay that way until it was all over, until all of the gunfire had ceased. They had been ambushed, and he had no way of knowing how many of his guys were down. He had to get back to camp. He took a deep breath and licked his lips. His mouth felt chalky and tasted of salt. He needed water. They had water back at camp.

When he thought the coast was clear, he stood and looked around for any fallen allies. Just then an explosion sounded and catapulted him into the air, tossing him several feet away, where he landed with a hard thud.

When he opened his eyes, his vision was blurred, and he was lost in a mental fog. He could no longer hear the sound of gunfire, but his ears were filled with a loud, harsh ringing. He attempted to move as knew he must get out of the war zone if he wanted to survive, but his body felt like it weighed a thousand pounds.

Was he hurt? He had no way of knowing. He was numb from fear and too stunned to successfully assess the damage. It appeared his body was still intact, so that was a good sign.

Just then a vision appeared, and Daniel thought he was receiving his very own guardian angel. His best friend and member of his team, Mike Bradford, towered over him.

Daniel was still unable to move, but he attempted to raise his hand to have Mike assist him to his feet.

Although the ringing in Daniel's ears had dulled slightly, he still could not make out what Bradford was saying to him. But suddenly it struck him as odd that Mike was not attempting to help get him up. Was he more hurt than he realized?

"Mike," he managed to croak out. "Help me, please."

As he stared into the eyes of his best friend and fellow soldier, Daniel saw Mike raise his gun. Daniel stared down the barrel. Suddenly understanding that the situation he was in was much worse than he could have ever imagined, Daniel asked, "Why?"

"Because I'm the hero in this story," Mike answered.

Before Daniel could even register the betrayal, Mike pulled the trigger on his own man.

A few moments later the screen went black, and the credits rolled. The audience sat in stunned silence, and some even wiped away tears.

When the lights turned on, it took a while before everyone's solemn mood could shift, and Dax held his breath.

"Well, Dax, congratulations. That was some of your best work yet. You should be proud of your performance," his agent, Maggie Mayfield said excitedly. "This will no doubt be a hit at the box office, and you, my friend, are my new favorite client. You're going to make us a lot of money."

As they left the crowded theater, cameras flashed obnoxiously, and reporters yelled his name. He flashed a megawatt smile to avoid taking a bad picture.

"Daxton Knight, how does it feel to be Hollywood's new leading man?"

Knight stopped in his tracks. "It feels just as I imagined—pretty damn good."

CHAPTER 1

"Dax, where are you? We were supposed to have a meeting with the producers for *Redemption,* forty-five minutes ago."

"Shit." Dax swung his legs over the side of the bed. "I completely forgot."

"Come on, Knight, this is the third obligation you have missed or shown up late to in a week. You really do not want to start getting a reputation for being difficult to work with. You may be a rising star, but even the brightest stars eventually burn out," Maggie chastised him.

He grumbled something incoherent. "I wouldn't be missing things if I had someone in control of my calendar. My personal assistant up and quit on me."

"Rachel Montgomery?"

"That would be the one."

"She quit, you fired her, or she left with a broken heart?"

"Same difference, right? Besides she was getting kind of clingy for my tastes." Dax glanced over at the long naked legs peeking out from beneath the covers. "I can't really talk about it at the moment."

"Hmm, Zola's there, isn't she? Did you two party too hard last night?"

"How did you know about her?"

"Oh, please, I have eyes and ears everywhere. Besides, someone leaked it to *Entertainment Tonight*. If I had to guess it was the skinny little model herself. Getting her name out there certainly wouldn't hurt her street cred."

Dax walked away so, on the off chance Zola was awake, she wouldn't be able to hear. "Are you able to hold the producers off until I can get there? Depending on traffic, I can be there in twenty minutes."

"I'll do my best, and you and I both know that on a good day it will still take at least thirty, so put on a clean shirt and get your ass in gear. We really need to get you a new assistant. Heaven forbid you should be in control of your own schedule. You're really making a mess of things for yourself, and more importantly, for me."

Dax smiled as his agent berated him. "I'm working on it. Maybe I should hire a man next time."

"Or, here's a thought that I know is completely out

of the realm of possibility—you could always try not sleeping with her."

"You know when I see a pretty girl, it's just hard for me to resist. I appreciate a woman's beauty and—"

"Yeah, yeah. You're a horn dog, I get it. My feelings are hurt that you've never tried anything with me," Maggie said in mock disgust.

They both knew that she was kidding, considering she was happily married with a kid in college and another one about to make her a grandmother.

"Oh, Maggie, you know it's not for lack of me trying. Besides, you're much too valuable to me. You're the only woman besides my mother, God rest her soul, who has been indispensable to me."

Maggie chuckled. "You are a smooth talker, I'll give you that, but flattery will get you nowhere, now hurry up."

She hung up on him as he uncapped the toothpaste and searched for eye drops to get rid of the redness that had accumulated from lack of sleep. As he gargled and rinsed, feminine arms wrapped around his neck.

"Were you going to leave without saying good-bye?" Zola's voice purred in his ear.

"Of course not," he lied. "You looked so peaceful that I didn't want to wake you. I was going to leave a note. I'm late for an important meeting."

"A note?" She pouted. "Is that all that last night earned me?"

She was referring to their wild romp in the hay, which Dax was surprised she even remembered because they were both fairly intoxicated.

"Oh, don't be like that." He gave her a quick kiss on her full lips. "It may have earned you a repeat performance later. But I've really got to go. I'm already late, and Maggie will have my head if I push her buttons any further. My personal assistant quit, and I'm not doing a great job of staying organized. I'm in the market for a new assistant"

"Well, Rachel had to go. She may have been your personal assistant, but she was taking up way too much of your personal time, if you ask me."

"How did you know about Rachel?"

"Darling, when a woman is interested in a man, she makes it her business to know who he spends time with." She ran her fingers through his hair. "And in case you needed reminding, I'm not the kind of girl you call disposable."

Zola opened the silk robe revealing her tall, thin physique. She parted her legs ever so slightly and helped his hand find her moist and ready center.

He groaned as the bulge in his jeans hardened. "I really can't be late. This will have to wait until later. And I was just kidding with Maggie about dispensable women. Do not take it to heart."

"I don't take many things to heart, Dax. The world I work in is one of the most fierce and competitive there is, and I'm at the top of my game. So if one of us is disposable—" She paused for effect and rubbed herself against the tight bulge in his pants. "Well, let's just say that with both of our careers sky rocketing and our amazing good looks, we just make sense together, lover."

"I do not disagree," Dax said as he kissed her quickly. "But I've got to go. Will you be here when I get back so we can pick up where we left off?"

"I doubt it. Zola waits for no man, but—" she said, smiling, lightening the mood, "—you can call me later."

As Dax walked out the door of his penthouse apartment, she called out. "Dax, it wouldn't hurt matters if you made sure the next assistant was unattractive."

Dax dodged the reporters as he unlocked the door to his Porsche and slid into the driver's seat. He revved the engine and prepared to put the car in gear. When he pulled down the visor to block out the California sun, a piece of paper fell out in his lap. He frowned in confusion as he knew the envelope was not there the last time he drove the car.

He opened it, distracted, as he tried to maneuver out of the parking garage. He stopped at the exit, waiting for the arm bar to rise to allow him out of the garage.

The message was short, but it was more the blood red coloring that caught his attention. It said in bold letters.

LIFE IMITATES ART. SAY GOODBYE, DANIEL SAMPSON.

"What the hell?"

He looked around at his surroundings, realizing that whoever left this ominous message was most likely not hiding in the garage watching him read it. A car honked its horn behind him, indicating he was wasting precious time just sitting idle.

Dax waved his hand in apology and peeled out angrily. It was just a foolish prank. Some delusional psycho fan who took hate mail one step further. He had a wide fan base and, before *Sampson's Soldie*r, it consisted of mostly women, but after the true story war film, men and patriots alike boarded the Dax Knight train.

One could not just have crowds of adoring screaming fans without bringing out a looney toon or two. It was not uncommon that some of these followers would even yell out the name of some of his characters instead of his own real name when trying to get his attention. They related to the characters, especially when it was a real life drama.

People experienced some of the things he portrayed in his acting. In their eyes, they were comrades. He had might as well have been in the trenches with some of the real war heroes as they stopped him to swap stories and pat him on the back. Some of them showed him their purple hearts or even their battle wounds, some of which he would have rather not seen. But he listened graciously because they had put their lives on the line and fought for freedom.

He played a role for entertainment, and, although

some of the scenes were pretty heavy, when the director yelled cut, Dax was free to go about his daily life and enjoy the things that everyone took for granted.

The guns being fired on set did not house real bullets. The bomb that knocked him off of his feet was actually a practiced move with a stunt instructor and special effects, and, even then, if ever he felt unsafe, he could call in a stunt double, and no one would be the wiser.

Dax was never in any real danger, but so many others were, so he did not consider it a nuisance to engage in conversation with his devoted fans. But along with all of the positive feedback, he had gotten a small amount of negative criticism as well.

Some military extremist thought he was a pretty boy who did not deserve the honor of wearing the uniform, even if it was just a costume for him. Dax had expected that not everyone was always going to think he was the most fantastic thing since sliced bread, but he just hoped that the good outweighed the bad.

Until now, he had considered himself lucky and remarkably unscathed, as all of his messages arrived via snail mail, to his website, or other social media outlets. This was the first time that a message had been delivered personally.

Dax didn't consider himself a wuss, but he would be lying to himself if he did not admit that it unnerved him. Part of it was the message itself, but the other thing bothering him was that whoever left the note had access to his car and was audacious and daring enough to leave it for him.

"There sure are some neurotic maniacs out there."

Dax pulled into the parking lot of the studio just as Maggie called his cell, breaking into his thoughts.

"Yes, I'm walking in now."

ഗ്ദ

Sonny Winslow sat at her writing desk and pecked away at the keyboard. She had been at this chapter for hours, trying to get it just right. She needed to tie in all of her plot twists to complete her manuscript.

The words flowed out of her like paint on a canvas as she perfected what she hoped would be the next great American novel. A potential publishing company was anxiously awaiting the long-talked about novel, and she knew she had to strike while the iron was hot.

The only problem was that the bills did not quit coming in while she took this time for herself to write. She had published smaller stories, but as a first time author of a novel, getting an advance was almost out of the question.

Sonny had tried to earn enough money by waitressing and being an expert barista at the local Artist Corner, but she was barely making ends meet between rent, utilities, and groceries.

One day, she would get a real paycheck for her time

spent in front of a keyboard, and her hard work would pay off, but until then, she would dread opening every envelope, knowing another bill was coming due.

She enjoyed being around other aspiring artists and writers at the Artist Corner. It was an inspiration to watch like-minded people working at their dreams, and the owner, Vivian Whitman, was motivation in her own right. She had opened the small art gallery and coffee shop on a whim and had done very well for herself. This allowed her to support local talent, along with some big names. She had become a mentor to Sonny and, after taking a liking to her, had offered her a job. Sonny had begun running her work past her for a second opinion as she finished each chapter. Only then was she planning to submit it to any agents. When she looked at the clock now, she realized she had to hurry in order to make their afternoon coffee date.

She printed out the final chapter before grabbing her purse. Vivian had been hounding her for weeks to read the latest installment of *Seize the Night.* It was a rough draft, but if she could overlook the errors, she may have some useful edits in mind that could help Sonny put the book to rest.

Sonny was already plotting her next mystery romance and couldn't wait to begin building her characters. They already existed through her imagination, and she was ready to bring them to life. In a strange sense, these characters were her friends. They needed a voice and, through Sonny, their stories could be shared.

She drove with the windows down, feeling free as her hair whipped around in the wind. She sang along to the song “Life is a Highway” before pulling into her usual parking space. Sonny waved absently to a few familiar faces, slinging her crossover bag, which held her newly printed pages, across her shoulder.

When she stepped inside the building, she saw Vivian waiting at a table, and she smiled pleasantly. Vivian started to stand to greet her, but given her very pregnant condition, Sonny waved her off, urging her to remain seated.

“How are you feeling? You look great.”

“Oh, baby is very active today, kicking up a storm.” Vivian placed a hand lovingly on her growing bump. “But otherwise, I feel great, as big as a whale, but that just means baby is growing and healthy.”

“Well, you look positively radiant. It must be true that babies make you glow. Or maybe it’s the life of a newlywed that has you beaming.”

“Both are great. The nursery is finally finished, and I have just about gotten everything unpacked in the new house.”

“I envy you,” Sonny said, smiling. “A beautiful family, a handsome new husband, and the steal you got on your new home. I’m so happy for you.”

"Thank you, Sonny. I am truly blessed. Miles is the best man that I could ask for. He puts up with my mood swings and impromptu tears as if it was completely normal and there is nothing else in the world he would rather do. He has picked up the extra duties of caring for a five-year-old without me asking. He is truly a gem, but it was hard work getting to the point in my life to meet him."

Sonny knew Vivian's history was not an easy one to overcome, but it gave her hope that happiness was out there for everyone.

"The saying that all things happen for a reason is true. Even if we don't always understand them at the time."

"Cheers to that." Vivian lifted her decaffeinated green tea. "I ordered you a latte, don't worry, no decaf for you, but this baby does not need anything else revving it up today. So, do you have the pages?" she asked anxiously. "I'm dying to know if Whitley and Wren end up together."

"Yes, I brought the pages. Please be kind, it's very rough. I finished it right before I came here."

"You know I don't care about a few typos. That's what editors are for. Your job, my dear, is getting the story on paper. We will worry about comma placement later."

Sonny smiled as she handed over her latest work.

"I cannot wait to relax in bed and take this all in," Vivian said. "But, Sonny, what is bothering you? Are you not happy with the ending? If you aren't ready for me to read it, I can wait."

"No, it's not that." Sonny sighed. "It's just, bills. Until I start getting paid for my writing, I still need to find a way to live. I have thought about getting a roommate to help with the rent, but finding someone with whom you are compatible to share your house with isn't always easy. I appreciate all that you have done by giving me a job, but, unfortunately, it isn't leaving much wiggle room."

"Say no more," Vivian assured her. "You're speaking to a friend, not your current employer. You think I don't realize that being a barista is not your ideal set up? I just wanted to help get you by. Don't get me wrong, I love having you here, but you're cut out for bigger and better things. One day soon, that thing will be being a full time author, but the industry is cutthroat."

"Tell me about it," Sonny groaned.

"Wait a minute." Vivian perked up. "I have an idea. I don't know why it just now occurred to me. I have made contacts in the industry through various conferences and events. There's one woman I became rather friendly with, Maggie Mayfield. She's an acting agent, and she represents Daxton Knight."

"Didn't he just release a new movie?"

"Yes, *Sampson's Soldiers.* Anyway, she informed me that he is starting to film a new movie, and he'll be relocated to Jerseyville. He is in need of a personal assistant. Maggie says the kid has great acting skills, but is a real scatterbrain. He needs someone to help control his schedule."

"Me? Be an assistant to Dax Knight? I don't know the first thing about what that entails."

"No, but I bet you could learn, and I'm sure it would pay a pretty penny. You might even get to rub some shoulders with the big wigs and be able to give them a copy of your manuscript. It wouldn't have to be a forever job, just while he's filming in our area. That might be long enough for an agent to get a publishing house to buy your book, and then all of your free time can be spent writing. It sounds perfect, the more I think about it."

"Yes, maybe too perfect. They probably won't hire someone who doesn't have experience."

"Before you throw in the towel, let me make a phone call for you. In the meantime, I have the perfect room-mate for you."

"Who?" Sonny asked dubiously.

Vivian indicated with a tilt of her head toward the hunk that was seated at the corner booth. He was writing feverously in a note pad.

"Another writer? I think I only have room for one of those in my house."

"Oh, come on. Be open minded. His name is Hudson Law. He dabbles in the arts, sells some paintings, but is trying his hand at writing. You have a lot in common and would probably understand each other's idiosyncrasies.

Splitting room and board would benefit you both. Plus, he is not bad to look at."

"I don't know anything about the man."

Although Vivian was right—he was easy on the eyes which, to Sonny, meant it was all the more intimidating.

"Miles has enough friends on the police force to make it easy to run a background check."

"You're just full of answers today," Sonny said. "You're lucky that you're pregnant."

Vivian smiled sweetly and held up Sonny's manuscript. "Do as your book says, and *Seize the Night.*"

Sonny rolled her eyes but laughed. She had to admit Vivian had her there.

CHAPTER 2

Sonny sat at the airport terminal nervously picking imaginary lint off of her linen trousers. She smoothed her wrinkleless blouse that she had steamed to perfection and crossed and uncrossed her high-heeled-clad feet.

She had splurged on the business suit at a sale at Macy's, trading in her normal coffee-stained attire for something a little more formal. She doubted that her normal cutoffs, soft fitted tees, and Converse would have landed her the job or impressed the actor.

After doing some research and seeing that he was recently dating Zola Wallace, the well-known face of Calvin Klein as well as walking the runway for all the designers during fashion week, Sonny had decided that Zola made jeans and going topless seem way more fashion forward than her new fitted suit.

The women he was used to had outfits tailor made specifically for their measurements and were offered this season's trends before they were ever sold in stores. She, on the other hand, had begrudgingly handed over her credit card to purchase last season's hand me downs.

Sonny was aware that she was anything but hideous, and most men appreciated her good looks and easy going style, but most men were not successful actors who were recently catapulted into fame with women throwing themselves at him.

She wasn't here for him to interview her based on her looks, she reminded herself. She was here to make money and find her book the right home. She wasn't as optimistic about her chances as Vivian had said Maggie Mayfield was, but Sonny would give it her best shot. What did she have to lose?

At the very least if it didn't work out, Hudson was moving into her guest room at the end of the week. Financially, that would take off some of the recent strain she had been feeling.

Lost in thought, she almost missed the crowd that had just de-boarded the plane. Shit, she thought as she hurried to her feet and grabbed the sign that said Daxton Knight in big letters.

Sonny spotted the man easily as he looked around expectantly from behind his aviator sunglasses. He wore a simple white tee with a light leather jacket and snug worn-on-purpose-looking jeans. He fit the part of "I didn't have to try, I just rolled out of bed looking like this" perfection.

She took a deep breath and stepped forward with her measly hand-written sign. "Mr. Knight?"

He turned to look at her and lifted his glasses momentarily. She shifted uncomfortably beneath his gaze and felt even more inept when he took in her noticeable self-made sign.

"You are here for the assistant job?" he asked suspiciously.

"Um, yes. I'm Sonny Winslow." She wiped her damp hand on her pant leg before offering it out to him.

He looked at it cautiously for a moment before accepting it. "You don't look like you have done this before," he commented speculatively.

"That's because I haven't," she answered honestly. "But you're in need of an assistant, and I'm willing to learn," she said brightly.

"What makes you want this job?" he asked, staring at her inquisitively.

"Well, I need a job, and my current employer thought this would be a good fit, as did your agent, Maggie. I'm sure I can be a great help to you if you give me a chance." She remained enthusiastic in her speech, but her heart was thudding in her chest.

"So you have a job, but are looking for a career change? Can I ask what is it that you do?"

"Well, I'm a waitress. I work at the local coffee shop and art gallery."

He started to roll his eyes.

"Well, that's not entirely correct. I do work there, but I'm primarily a writer. I need a better paying job until my book deal goes through. I figured I could assist you while you're working in the area, and—"

"And use me to get your book published," he finished for her.

"N—No, of course not," she stammered. "I mean if it worked out that would be wonderful," she admitted. "But that's not my sole purpose. I need a job, and this happened to be available."

"Let's get my bags," he said without further ado.

As they walked to baggage claim, she struggled to find something to say. "Look, Mr. Knight, I know that you're probably used to people wanting something from you and riding on your coat tails, but that just isn't me. I work hard for all that I have, and this job will be no different. One day, I'll be a published writer, and I do not need you to do it."

He stopped walking and turned to face her with raised eyebrows. "We'll do this on a trial basis. If you're the perfect assistant, then you can continue. I don't care what you do in your free time, write to your heart's content, but I need someone committed to my busy schedule."

She nodded her understanding. "Of course."

"Now, we all have to ride coat tails at some point to get to where we're going, and I don't necessarily mind being a bridge for opportunity, but I also only want my name attached to things I believe in. So if and when we get to that point, I will decide then."

"Yes, Mr. Knight. I'm only asking for a job, not for your name to be associated with my novel."

"Oh, I see. You don't want my name to overshadow your work?"

She sighed in exasperation. "Why do I get the feeling you're trying to trip me up?"

"Relax, Ms. Winslow. I'm just feeling you out."

She reddened ever so slightly, and he wondered if it was because she was angry.

"And how am I measuring up?" she asked.

"I haven't decided yet, but I'll let you know when I do."

Dax turned toward the carousel and swore. "Damn, we missed my bag. We will have to wait for it to come back around."

Sonny sat silently wondering if this was really a good idea after all.

ᔕᔓᔕᔓ

Sonny drove the rental car, paying careful attention to the navigating system, aware that any mistake would discredit her further. "Where to first, Mr. Knight?"

"Did you receive an email of all of my engagements?"

"Yes, Maggie had them sent to me. She left room for jet lag, so you have the afternoon free. Are you hungry or did you need to stop somewhere?"

"No, just show me to the house, and I'll unpack."

"Okay, some of your things were already sent, and I took the liberty of picking up some of your favorite foods."

He gave her a look, wondering how she knew anything about his favorite anything.

"Maggie sent me a list."

"Of course she did. So will I dig my new residence or what?"

"Oh, yes, I think you will be very pleased. It's a new villa, and everything in it's top of the line, very sleek. You must be used to those sorts of things, though. I'm sure it will be to your standards."

"Standards? You don't agree with enjoying the finer things in life?"

"No, I have no problem with that at all. I didn't meant to insinuate—"

"That I was an over-privileged snot?"

"Not at all. That's not what I meant."

He laughed. "Relax. You need to learn not to take the bait. I'm an expert fisherman."

"No, you're annoying and argumentative." The words flew out of her mouth before she could stop them.

"See, there you go." Dax smiled. "I lived in a trailer when I got my first acting gig, and I could barely afford Ramen noodles. The sooner you view me as a normal person, the better off we'll be. Besides, I'm not into hero worship."

"No need to worry about that, Mr. Knight," she said sarcastically.

"See? You're getting better already. Call me Dax."

ᘓᘐᘓᘐ

When Sonny left Dax's oversized apartment, she was exhausted. She had helped unpack him, run a few errands, and grocery shopped. She prepared his dinner, and he then excused himself to study his lines, and she had asked him if he needed anything else.

"No, Ms. Winslow. I think you've done enough for the day. Good job, I might add. I'm pleasantly surprised so far."

"I'm glad I've met your standards." She smiled her first genuine smile.

"You should do that more often."

"What? Surpass your expectations?"

"No, smile. It brightens up your whole face."

Her cheeks reddened again, and he took pleasure in making her uncomfortable.

"Uh, thank you. And as long as we're on a first name basis, call me Sonny."

"Sonny, I like the sound of that."

She cleared her throat. "So, will Ms. Wallace be joining you soon?"

"I see you have done your research. But, Zola, no. She's in Paris, promoting a new fragrance commercial. She won't be happy, though."

"Why's that?" she asked, alarmed.

"She wanted you to be ugly."

"Oh, I see." She did not know how to respond. "Well, sorry to disappoint. I guess I'll see you tomorrow."

"Yep, you've made it for another day. See you tomorrow, Sonny."

೧೨೧೨

Flirtations came easily to Dax. It was the only way he knew how to communicate with the opposite sex. And luckily for him, it usually worked in his favor. He enjoyed being inappropriate. Rarely were women put off by it. Usually, it was quite the opposite. They were flattered. He found that women enjoyed feeling good, feeling wanted and appreciated. If he stroked their ego, he could usually get whatever he wanted out of them.

He didn't claim to be a saint or even that he was morally that sound. He never even claimed to be a nice guy. Sometimes he could be a downright asshole, but he wasn't always a bad guy either, or at least he tried not to be.

Dax hadn't been overly kind today with Sonny, but he was already irritated that he was the last to know that his new assistant was inexperienced, and he already had a preconceived notion that working with her was going to be a headache.

He could admit when he was wrong, and so far, she had done all right. She went above and beyond with preparing food, setting up his apartment to his liking, organizing his dates on an easy-to-read calendar, and she even programmed his phone so that reminders would go off, and he would have no excuse to forget an obligation. So far, so good, and only time would tell.

Dax felt a twinge of guilt for giving her a hard time. He wasn't used to giving a damn about anything he did. Maybe it was the innocent way she had pleaded for him to give her a chance. There was a sweetness or wholesomeness to her.

It was obvious in the way that she filled his place with fresh flowers, vanilla-scented candles, and had baked his favorite cookies of macadamia nuts. Dax was used to women doing stuff for him, but usually because they wanted something from him. This girl just wanted to work to make some money, and he could respect that. She made him aware that she would not swallow her pride and be walked on to do it, though, and he could admire that.

Besides, she was cute—no, more than just cute—but in the opposite way that Zola was attractive. Sonny was short, compact, more of an athletic build, but had an ample bust—a little more than a handful, judging with his expert eye. She wore a stylish bob with low-key umber highlights, probably so that she could skip a coloring if funds were tight, and it would go mostly unnoticed. She had a soft sprinkling of freckles across her face that were more pronounced when she wrinkled her nose disapprovingly, which he found that she did often throughout the day.

Zola was out-right sexy, that much was obvious. All you had to do was take a look at her seductive poses for her ads. She was tall, rail thin, with perky breasts that rarely required her to wear a bra. She wore her glossy, dark hair long, and it was luscious and thick, due to a head full of extensions.

She had dark eyes and the cream tan complexion to match. She was labeled exotic by magazines, and her sex appeal sizzled like a spicy enchilada. Thinking of Zola, he should probably call her. What was the time difference? She was about seven hours ahead. She would probably be sleeping and, in all honesty, he did not really feel like hearing about the fashion world when he was trying to go to bed. So, instead, he read ahead on his lines and drifted to sleep.

ԑ϶ԑ϶

Dax awoke the next morning to the smell of coffee brewing. He groaned when he looked at the clock. His brain might not have been awake, but below his waste was, so he had to give it a minute before he got up. When his flag went down to half-staff, he was satisfied he wouldn't be too crude walking out to the kitchen, so he threw some sweat pants on and quickly brushed his teeth.

He opened the French doors to his bedroom and saw Sonny bustling around the kitchen.

"You're here early."

"Yeah, I wasn't sure what time you wanted to get started, and by the time I got home, it was too late to call. I figured you might be sleeping after all of the travel. I thought if you weren't awake, I would make breakfast and start answering some of your mail. If you wanted me to, that is."

"Yes, great plan."

She handed him a cup of coffee and tried to avoid looking at his shirtless torso. He was lean and muscular. He had to train constantly for his role as a lieutenant in the army. His skin was virtually smooth and hairless, excluding the small patch below his navel leading to the top of low riding sweat pants.

She looked away, hoping he wouldn't notice what had distracted her. "Well, the muffins will be done in just a couple of minutes, and the bacon and eggs are in the warmer."

"Muffins, what kind?"

"Blueberry."

"Those are my favorite."

She gave him a knowing look.

"Of course, you already know that. How can I remain a man of mystique and complexity when my agent reveals every intricate detail?"

"If you think that your mysteriousness has been jeopardized over some muffins, then you've got bigger issues. Besides, your secrets are safe with me."

He smiled at her quick wit. "I have a feeling you're going to keep me on my toes."

"I have a feeling you need someone to keep you in line," Sonny said, being blatantly honest.

"That may be true," Dax admitted. "And that's what you are getting paid to do."

"Oh, a glorified babysitter is my actual job title? I was unaware. I thought I was getting paid to be on top of a busy professional's schedule," she teased. "I guess I better get to some of your adoring fan mail, so that no one finds out how unorganized you truly are."

"My publicist usually handles most of that, but go ahead, open some. Let's see what the Dax Fan Club has to say. I could use a little uplifting this morning. So far it's been a tough crowd."

"Oh, poor Daxton Knight, can't handle a woman who has a little personality, much less an opinion?"

She laughed as she slid her finger through the seal.

"Actually, I prefer a woman who has a brain in her head. If you can write a decent book, I would assume you do."

"Who said my book was decent?"

"You don't think that it is?" he countered.

"I didn't say that. I'm just saying you have no idea whether it is or it isn't."

"True, but, Sonny, the first step in getting someone else to believe in your work is believing in it yourself. You have to be able to sell, not only the book, but yourself. You seem confident enough—"

"Dax."

"What? Is that just a front?"

"No, look at this," she said, indicating the piece of paper she just pulled out of the envelope.

"What? Is it a nude? Sometimes my fans go above and beyond."

"What about your haters? What do they do?"

"What are you talking about?"

She handed him the pages, obviously taken aback. Dax read and reread before slowly meeting her questioning gaze.

"Well, is this common?" she asked.

He attempted to shrug it off nonchalantly. "No, not really."

"What do you mean, not really? I mean, I barely know you, but so far you don't strike me as a man of few words. You like to talk, maybe too much sometimes. So what gives? This person obviously was near enough to get that close up of a picture, and you obviously had no idea it was being taken. And the message says 'Daniel Sampson, you are never alone. I can see to your demise whenever I so choose. Spend your last days wisely.'"

"Thank you for the recap. I wasn't aware that I could not read," Dax said crisply.

"I wasn't trying to be a smartass, but who takes the time to cut out each letter separately from magazines? I thought they only did that in ransom movies. And who is Daniel Sampson? Wasn't that your character in your last movie?"

Dax rolled his eyes. "Yes, he was. He was also a person in real life. I played his role in the major blockbuster movie, *Sampson's Soldiers*. Maybe you have seen it?"

Sonny lowered her eyes and was saved by the oven timer going off, indicating that the muffins were ready. She busied herself with finding oven mitts.

"You have seen it, haven't you?"

She raised her eyes sheepishly. "It was on my list of things to do, I swear."

"Wow, I see where I rank. That's enough to humble a man. Out of millions of Americans, my own employee hasn't seen my movie."

Sonny stifled a laugh. "I'm glad we did not have this conversation yesterday when I was begging for a job. I'm guessing that wouldn't have scored me any points. If it makes you feel any better, I have heard it was very good."

"Yeah, let's hope the academy agrees."

"We're on the heels of award season, aren't we? But let's quit avoiding the question at hand. You said that you don't really receive hate mail like this, so it doesn't concern you? I mean, this could be considered a death threat and should be taken seriously."

"People can be hateful. Usually, when I'm being bashed, it's from someone's Twitter account, or they'll just blog about it. People can feel really big and bad from behind a keyboard, and they really pull out the big guns when they remain anonymous. The part that's strange is how I received the message, and—" He hesitated. "—this isn't the first one like it."

"Continue, don't keep me hanging," Sonny urged.

"There was a note that was left above the visor in my car. I can't be sure how long it was left there."

Dax went into his bedroom and retrieved the threat from his nightstand. He handed the menacing words to Sonny.

"'Life imitates Art. Say goodbye, Daniel Sampson.' What the hell, Dax? Do you think that this is from the same person?"

"I have absolutely no idea. I would be inclined to say no, except in both instances, I'm referred to as my character's name. I'm sure it's just a tasteless prank. Someone who feels I did not do Lieutenant Sampson justice."

"Well, what an awful way to express their opinion. In both messages, you're being threatened."

"I don't take any of that too seriously. There are a lot of whack jobs out there."

"Well, that's reassuring. As long as it's just the ramblings of a mentally unstable person." Her voice dripped with sarcasm. "Doesn't your character die at the end of the movie?"

"I guess you'll have to watch to find out."

She tilted her head in exasperation.

He sighed. "Yes, spoiler alert, Daniel Sampson dies in battle, at the hands of one of his own men."

She raised her eyebrows. "Interesting."

"Don't go over thinking things. This is not the plot for your next book. It's nothing."

She relented. "Okay, if you say so. What's on the agenda for today?"

"I have to run lines. We start shooting tomorrow, and I've put off rehearsing until the last minute."

"That seems to be a recurring theme with you. Why don't you eat for some brain fuel before you start?"

"Yes, ma'am. You don't have to tell me twice."

"But, Dax, you are wrong about one thing."

"What's that?"

"You obviously took the first note seriously enough that you kept it."

"That's the writer in you. Don't read too much into it."

CHAPTER 3

Parker Maxwell had the world at his fingertips and carried a certain air of confidence about him. Men who knew him wanted to be with him, and ladies who saw him wanted to be with him. Life could not have been better.

Most people who encountered him thought that he was a lucky bastard and fate must have smiled down on him. He was blessed with good looks, impossible charm, and was climbing the charts with his latest *New York Times* best seller.

No one would guess the hard work and rejections it had taken to get there. To them, it seemed like everything Parker touched turned to gold, with the exception of many a woman's broken heart along the way. That did not stop the young bachelorettes from trying, but he wasn't in the market for a wife.

He had seen what married life could do to a man. It slowed them down, aged them, and made them incapable of making a decision on their own. No, he wasn't in the business of saying, "Yes, dear, whatever you say, dear."

He had tried to warn his buddies before they took the big leap, but most had not listened for fear of winding up alone.

But was that really so bad? He lived his life for himself, went and did as he pleased, and that had suited him just fine. If he wanted to stay up all hours of the night in a writing frenzy, he did just that. He had no one nagging him the next day to get out of bed. The only person he answered to was his agent, and that was annoying enough. But she was the one who got him the deals, had helped him make the big bucks. So he didn't complain too much when she came calling.

Most of all, he wasn't tied down to one woman for the rest of his life. He was free to see and sleep with whoever he wanted. And he did just that—tasted and roamed the waters. When he tired of one, he moved on to the next. Very rarely did his conscience not approve of the decisions he made.

He had watched some of the buddies he had tried to warn go through a nasty divorce, and he would say, "I told you so," over a cold one as they poured their heart out. Women could be vultures.

Parker was not a woman hater. He loved women—just in the plural sense and never the singular. If he started to enjoy one lady friend's company too much, he moved on to the next as quickly as possible.

His money was his, his life style was his, and he intended for it to stay that way. Parker had watched other friends procreate, and that was fine for them. He didn't hate kids. But he could not imagine his expensive clothing being covered in snot and drool. His friends talked about their kid's goal during a soccer game like it was the newest Victoria Secret's model serving them an icy beverage from between her lacy-braziered, silicone-filled tits. He could respect that. It just wasn't the life for him.

He sat pondering this over a single malt scotch in the middle of the afternoon by himself. Parker had just finished his latest novel and sported three days' worth of stubble on his normally clean shaven face. He had been holed up in his penthouse apartment, writing feverously, until the grand finale. In some ways, the release of finishing the book was better than climaxing during sex. It sure was a hell of a lot more work.

The characters were never far from his mind, urging and begging to be able to come out of the box he had filed them away in, in his brain. After finishing his story, one of two things happened. He was either physically spent or on an adrenaline high.

Today, he was on a long-awaited high, and that was when he saw them. A group of women came in cackling on a bachelorette party. They were getting an early start and looked dressed up and put together. He would bet any amount of money that, in a few hours from now, it would be a different story.

They would be stumbling around a dance floor, allowing sleazy men to buy them shots and, inevitably, at least one of them would end up crying in the bathroom. The F-bombs would fly, and the class and sophistication they put off would all but diminish, along with the tracks of their supposedly water-proof mascara. He had seen this crowd before, maybe not these particular women, but they were all the same.

Just as he was thinking to himself that if you had seen one, then you had seen them all, there was one woman who stood out in the crowd. She was an exquisite sight, and her smile lit up the room. She was blonde with big pearly white teeth and a laugh that sounded like angels singing. He was caught in the melody and enchanted, but when she picked up her drink, he noticed the sparkling diamond on her third finger of her left hand.

Parker was mildly disappointed but decided without hesitation that if he didn't buy her a drink, that would simply be discriminating against all the beautiful married, or about to be married, women. That ruled out a large percentage of the female population and who was he to judge their life choices? Besides, put simply, he viewed it as a challenge and, as far as he was concerned, everything was negotiable.

Parker walked over to the barstool where she and some friends had set up camp. She was the last of the group to notice the intrusion. By that point, one of the other girls had already started eyeing him with interest. Vultures, he thought, wryly. The singles in this party were trying to join their friends in holy matrimony by husband shopping. He felt sorry for their desire for commitment and, ultimately, their desperation.

"Hello, ladies, don't tell me your lucky men let you out of their sight for the night."

The two women, who accompanied the one that had captured his interest, giggled.

"We're out for a bachelorette party," they squealed.

Duh, he thought. "Oh, that's exciting. I was just about to ask if I could buy this lovely lady a drink." He eyed the woman in his best you-know-you-want-me-to look.

"No, thank you. I already have a drink," she answered smoothly.

"Oh, come on, Bev. Let him buy you a drink," the girls chanted.

"Yeah, come on, Bev, let me buy you a drink. What would you like? Let me guess, an apple martini, or sex on the beach?" He smiled a knowing smile.

"A beer." She relented with a sigh. "I'll take a simple beer, on draft, please, no foam."

"Be still my heart, a woman who drinks draft beer."

"I also eat hot wings with my hands and don't starve myself," she quipped.

"All the qualities I look for in a woman," Parker said.

"Oh, I bet you say that to all of the girls."

He smiled as he handed her the beer. "So what is your full name?"

"Does it matter?" she asked without missing a beat.

"It does to me," he said truthfully.

"Her name is Beverly Litchfield," her friend answered for Beverly and then said, "and my name is Robin Taylor."

"Well, it's nice to meet you both. So who's the poor woman who's going to get entirely too intoxicated, do something she regrets, and then jump off a bridge with the other poor souls, and say I do?"

"Nice to know there are still some people who believe in true love out there in the world," Beverly said with irony.

"I'm a realist. What can I say? So who is the bride to be?"

She turned her chair to stand up and said, "That would be me."

His mouth dropped open slightly.

"Thanks for the beer."

"Parker," he said as she walked away. "My name is Parker."

ര൭ര൭

"Oh, this is getting good." Sonny sat with her feet

tucked up underneath her, reading the back story of Dax's new movie, *For Better or Worse.*

"You think so? Some would say it's a cheesy love story," Dax said.

"It's quite different from the story line that you described for your previous movie, but I think it shows your diversity as an actor and your ability to play many different roles. A lot of actors get caught up in one genre and can't shake the stigma of only being seen as one type of character."

"Yes, that's what I was thinking. *Sampson's Soldiers* was a very deep and involved role. I wanted something a little easier on the heart for my next job," Dax explained.

"Well, I think this movie will do just that. Besides who isn't a sucker for a happy ending?"

"Please don't tell me that. The world's full of real problems."

"Many people go to the movies to escape reality and want some feel-good entertainment."

"Is that what you look for in a movie?" Dax asked.

"Don't we all wish for easy at one point or another?" Sonny countered.

"What reality are you trying to escape?"

"Me, nothing, but it's nice to see a story that works out in the end. One where dreams can come true."

"Is that how your book ends? They lived happily ever after?" Dax asked quietly.

Sonny squirmed under his gaze.

"Why the discomfort? You don't like when the tables are turned, and you're asked about your work? If your book gets accepted, you'll have to be able to talk about it."

"I know. It's just so raw still. I literally just finished polishing it up. My characters are flawed, the story is not without heartbreak, and my people go through tribulations to find themselves, but ultimately, yes, I like to think it ends well and the way it was supposed to. That's all I will say. For more on how it ends you will just have to read it."

"I look forward to it," Dax said meaningfully.

"Really?" she asked, surprised.

"Of course. Remember, I told you I *am* capable of reading."

She laughed easily.

"There it is again."

"What?"

"The beautiful sound of laughter. I told you that you should do it more often."

They held a gaze for a second too long, and Sonny said, "Oh, I see you use your lines from your movies. Besides, maybe you should try being more funny, and I would laugh more."

Dax grinned. "I'll remember that."

ധൗധൗ

Sonny left that evening, feeling better about how the

job of being an assistant to Hollywood's leading it man was going. She was not nearly as intimidated as she had been when she picked him up from the airport. He really was just a human being doing a job, a very well-known media-scrutinized job.

She felt a kinship with him because they were both passionate about the arts, and at least that gave them some common ground. Still, she was nervously anticipating the next day when they would be on set together. He was the one who had to perform, but she had never assisted someone before and hoped she accomplished what was expected of her, especially since she had no clue what those expectations were.

Dax was flirtatious and ostentatious, but she did not read into his nonstop innuendos, and she also realized he did not know any other way to communicate. She shrugged off his vulgar language and open-ended questions with ease, and he did not seem to mind when she blatantly ignored his ridiculous insinuations.

She wondered if he was that way with Zola or any other woman he had dated, or if it was reserved for women he did not particularly have an interest in, as if they were just target practice. Either way, she understood it was a game to him, to see if he could get a rise out of her or ruffle her feathers. She had decided that he could not, and a line had been drawn.

Nevertheless, as soon as she had taken her stance and drawn it, he had done his best to cross it. In his profession, she was sure he was used to everyone reciprocating anything he put their way. She was just as sure that if he thought she would have reciprocated, he wouldn't have done it. Many men were like that. They enjoyed playing cat and mouse. In her mind, it was perfectly okay to play the role of the mouse, as long as you knew you were really the cat.

When she was almost back to her humble abode, she realized she had a missed call from Hudson Law. She dialed him back quickly, activating her blue tooth in her car.

"Sonny?"

"Yes."

"Hey, it's Hud. I was wondering if it would be okay if I moved some of my things into the apartment tonight."

"Oh, yes, of course. You planned to move for good in a couple of days from now anyway. You might as well get an early start."

"Yeah, about that. I thought maybe I could just start saying at the apartment tonight. You see my girlfriend, now ex-girlfriend, and I shared a place, but she moved out to try to make it work with some other guy. Apparently, the grass wasn't green in either pasture, so she decided to move back in and plans to take over the lease. We would just as well rather not stay there together for the next couple of days. We haven't quite reached the friend zone, if you know what I mean."

"Oh, yes, I'm sure that could get messy." Sonny

didn't know how else to reply. She had no idea about his relationship issues. She barely knew him at all. "I'm actually turning onto my street now. You're welcome to come by anytime."

When she rounded the corner, she saw Hudson with a big pickup truck in front of her residence.

"I took a chance," he said, spotting her car. "I hope that you don't mind."

"No, it's no problem at all. I'll see you in a second."

Sonny found a parking spot on the street and worked to train her face to not show how taken off guard she was. She really did not mind. The move was going to happen sooner or later, but she wasn't prepared for it right this instant.

She greeted the man kindly. "Hey, I'm sorry you're going through a rough time. Vivian didn't tell me you were going through a break up."

"Yeah, I didn't really make it public knowledge, and I'm sorry to spring this on you."

"No, it's really no problem. Let me change, and I'll help you with your belongings."

"Thanks, I really appreciate this, by the way. I don't have much stuff, considering I let her have most of it in the unofficial custody battle. I was just done arguing by that point. The most important things are my laptop and a mattress. I'm sure you understand that, as a writer, I just need a place to work and a pillow to put under my head."

"Yeah, I get that," Sonny agreed.

"I mean, I'm not a gypsy. I'm legit. I'll pay my bills on time. Don't worry about that," he said quickly. "You're probably wondering what you got yourself into. I'm making myself seem like a complete mess."

"No, not at all," she reassured him. "Besides, I agreed to rent to you, based on the recommendation of Vivian and Miles. They have never steered me wrong before." She hesitated. "And Miles has friends in law enforcement, so we ran a background check on you."

Hudson laughed a deep manly laugh. It was warm and not at all the sound you would have expected to come out of someone you should be frightened by.

"I should have known. Well, I'm glad my clean record put you at ease."

He was handsome, in an unkempt, struggling-writer sort of way. His clothes were casual and worn down to the point of comfort, and his green eyes sparkled with a hint of mischievousness. Oh, boy, she thought. She went from seeing handsome characters in her mind that she struggled to capture on paper to two real life hunks right in front of her.

Sonny changed out of her work attire, began unloading boxes, and discovered that Hudson was right. His belongings were meager, to say the least. Still, she and Hud were tired from having to walk up the flight of stairs repetitively.

"I owe you big time," he said. "Do you want me to order a pizza?"

"I could eat a slice," she agreed.

After he had called in their order and she offered him a beer, he said, "So, you have a new job, working for Daxton Knight. What's he like?"

She pondered the question, not sure if she exactly knew the answer herself. "It's going well. At first, I thought he was going to be an egotistical asshole, and he kind of is, but it turns out he might be an easier person to work for than I had expected. Today was only day two on the job so I still have a lot to learn, but so far so good. He takes his work very seriously, and it's interesting to watch the process of movie making unfold. Tomorrow's our first day on set."

"I saw *Sampson's Soldiers*, and the guy gave a really moving performance. I'd like to meet him. I hear he's probably up for some awards."

Sonny felt herself fill with pride, although she had nothing to do with his previous success. "I'm sure you'll get the opportunity eventually."

Twenty minutes later, the pizza guy buzzed them to let him know he was there.

"I'll grab it. Be back in a flash," Hudson said.

When he left, she smiled at her good fortune. He was not a creep at all, and this set up would really benefit her financially. She needed to remind herself to thank Vivian for the recommendation.

When Hudson came back up with the pizza, he was wary and had a strange look on his face.

"What's wrong? Did they get the order wrong?"

"Uh, no," he said and showed her what was in his hand. "I think these are for you."

It was a bouquet of dead, wilted flowers with a ribbon intertwined around the dried up petals and baby's breath. On it read her name, *Sonny Winslow*. It was the kind of arrangement you would see at a funeral home.

With trembling hands, she reached for the card, and it read:

Any friends of Parker Maxwell is not a friend of mine.

I pick them off one by one like dead decaying flowers on a vine.

"What the hell? Who is Parker Maxwell?" Hudson asked.

"It's Daxton Knight's new character for his upcoming movie."

CHAPTER 4

Sonny had barely slept after receiving the disturbing message the night before. She had been so tempted to throw the dead bouquet into the trash, but she wanted to be able to show it to Dax to get his thoughts on it.

She had had to explain to Hudson about the previous hate mail that Dax had received. Needless to say, Hudson was more than a little taken aback by the degree of dislike that this deranged fan was expressing.

Sonny had no doubt that it was the same person behind all of the veiled threats, and the fact that they had now involved her had her more than a little worried. How did this obsessive person even know her or that she was working for Dax? And he or she also knew where she lived. It was obviously not a delivery person because the flowers had come after hours of any florist she knew. Not to mention a delivery service would most likely not deliver a disturbing present like that at all. The unwelcomed visitor must have waited until they were done unloading Hudson's things. She shuddered at the thought of them being watched.

Sonny arrived fifteen minutes ahead of schedule so that it would allow her time to discuss her unwanted present. She knocked on the door and rang the buzzer, only to receive silence. She grabbed her key and let herself in. The house was quiet, and she cursed Dax for not waking up to the alarm that she had set for him.

The third day on the job and she was walking uninvited into his bedroom. Good Lord. She nudged his shoulder gently. "Dax. It's time to get up."

"Mmm."

"Dax." She nudged him harder that time. "You don't want to be late."

Dax had his eyes closed and pulled her down on the bed by her waist.

"Dax," she said louder. "Quit messing around."

Suddenly, he nuzzled her neck and, before she could squirm away, his lips met hers. She was so taken off guard that, at first, she remained still, and, in shock. Dax grazed his lips lazily over hers as if he had done it a hundred times. He nipped her top lip playfully, and a tingle shot through her groin.

She shoved him hard against his chest. “Dax, I’m not Zola, it’s Sonny. Wake up from whatever wet dream you are having and get ready, dammit.”

Dax’s eyes flew open and took a second to focus on her. He glanced over at the alarm clock. “Shit, I must have turned it off in my sleep.”

He threw back the covers and showed no shame in being caught in his boxers. He turned to hide the fading erection that had prompted him to kiss her.

Dax rushed into the bathroom to take a five-minute shower while she could still feel the effects of his lips on hers. She brushed her fingertips over them in an imaginary attempt to wipe the awkward moment away.

“Hey, will you grab me an outfit? It doesn’t matter which one. I will be getting dressed by wardrobe later.”

She opened his closet and grabbed a clean white shirt and blue jeans, similar to what she had seen him wear the first day. She knocked on the bathroom door, and he opened it, wearing a towel and brushing his teeth. His body still glistened with droplets of water, and his muscles gleamed under the moisture.

“Here.” She handed him the clothes, prepared to turn away.

He spit into the sink. “No underpants?” he asked, smiling.

She blushed ferociously. “I wasn’t sure which drawer you kept them in.”

"If the thought of touching my under garments can make you go that red, I guess I'll just have to go commando."

Without a moment's hesitation, he whipped the towel from his hips, and Sonny turned, barely escaping an eye full. "Dax!"

"What? It's just the human body. You can turn around now. I promise I won't threaten your virtue with my naked manhood."

Sonny hesitated, turned around slowly, and saw that Dax stood completely clothed and grinning like the cat that ate the canary.

She swatted his arm. "You really are impossible, you know that?"

"So I've been told."

'Well, come on. I won't have you be late to your first day." She paused. "Holy crap, I sound like my mother. You really are the equivalent of a small child."

"Maybe you should spend the night, in case I have a bad dream." He wiggled his eyebrows.

"Did this work with your last assistant?"

Dax smiled wider.

"I figured as much, which would also be why you no longer had an assistant. Am I correct?"

"Point taken," he said.

"Good, now get your butt in the car."

"Yes, ma'am. But what about breakfast?"

She eyed him dangerously.

"Okay, I'll just eat the food on set," he said.

Sonny drove him to the set in silence. She was pondering whether she should tell him about the flower delivery or if she should just let it be until he was done working.

He was going over his lines and mumbling them under his breath. She did not want to interrupt him at work. He was in the zone, and she knew how that could be. If you were interrupted in the middle of a creative thought, sometimes there was no getting it back.

She decided it could wait as she flashed her parking badge and pulled into the lot closest to Dax's trailer. He looked up, seeing the location for the first time as he had been so deeply concentrating.

"Are you nervous?" she asked, sensing his energy.

"Just anxious anticipation. It's always like this on the first day or night before a big scene. Nervous energy, combined with artistic adrenaline which I use to make my performance more authentic. It's said that if you lose it, that's when you are ready to retire."

"Oh, good to know. Well, break a leg then, I guess."

"Are you okay? You seem quiet and distracted. Are you still uncomfortable about this morning?"

"What? No, you were half asleep. It's fine, like it never happened," she said nonchalantly as possible.

Dax grinned, getting ready to shut the car door. "Good, but how do you know that I wasn't really awake and just acting?"

ᘓᘐᘓᘐ

The man was frustrating. Handsome, but frustrating, Beverly Litchfield thought. He obviously thought he had a lot of game because this act had probably produced high success rates in the past, but she was engaged to be married.

Beverly was not into bachelorette parties or being made a fool of, but at the insistence of her friends, she had agreed. If she was honest, she had done it more for them than for herself. They had traveled all this way to celebrate her and Steven's wedding. As a bride, there were certain obligations, but she was uncomfortable being the center of attention.

Parker came up from behind her. "So why aren't you wearing the typical white veil, blinking lights, and plastic penises that usually accustom such events?"

She sighed. "That's not really my style."

"No, I guess not."

Parker had shown up randomly at their last three stops.

"Are you following us?" she asked coolly.

"No, of course not," he said in exaggerated offense. "I'm just a man out for a couple of drinks. So when are these impending nuptials to take place?"

"There is nothing impending about it. And in a few days from now, I'll be a married woman. A few of my bridesmaids flew in for the shower and bachelorette party."

"What's the lucky groom's name?"

She gave him a look of mild annoyance. "I'm not sure why you care, but his name is Steven. Steven Calvird."

"So you are to be Mrs. Calvird?"

"That's right," she said.

"Do you love him?"

"What kind of question is that?"

"It's a simple yes or no answer."

"I mean, of course, I love him. We're getting married."

"Yes, I caught that part. Did you love him before you said yes?"

"Look, Steven and I have been together for a long time. He's a very successful man, and it's really no business of yours."

"No, I suppose it's not, but most of the time brides at least seem a little more…excited…to land a man and get him on a leash."

"I'm excited. But we've been together long enough that it's just a formality. Nothing will really change. I have no desire to land a man or keep him on a short leash. If I wanted a dog, I would have gotten one. Why such sour views on the subject? Let me guess, some woman broke your heart and left you cynical and cold hearted?"

"It just isn't my thing. I mean, it's fine for other people, but I have seen it end badly for most that have tried it. Pardon me for saying so, but it does not appear to be your thing either."

"And pardon me for saying that you do not know me, so how would you know what is my thing?" she said, raising her voice.

"It's just that I've seen people in love before. I write about it. Women's eyes light up, and they gush and rave how excited they are about the future. You don't sparkle when you talk about…what was his name? …Steven."

"I don't sparkle, huh? What am I, a firecracker?"

"I bet you could be." Parker stared at her seriously, and she felt like she had walked into that one.

Beverly held his gaze and leaned forward. She tilted her head seductively. Close enough that he could feel her breath on his face. His breath hitched in his throat, and his pulse picked up a notch. He leaned in until they were almost nose to nose.

Beverly hesitated, leaving them intimately close without having contact. Then she grabbed his face, and he closed his eyes, waiting for their lips to meet.

Then she slowly turned his face and whispered in his ear. She annunciated every word. "You don't know me."

She stood swiftly off of her barstool and sauntered to the ladies' room. When she got out of the stall, she placed a call to Steven.

"Hey, babe, I thought we were supposed to have no contact tonight. You're out with your girls, I'm out with my boys."

"Yeah, I know. I just wanted to hear your voice."

"Aren't you having fun?"

"Yes, I am. I just wanted to see how your night was going," she said.

It was loud, and the reception was terrible. Steven shouted across the line.

"I'm sorry, babe, but they're calling for me. I have to go. Don't forget that Mother wants to go for another dress fitting and brunch tomorrow."

"I won't forget."

Of course, his mother always got what she wanted. She wanted to be involved in every aspect of their lives. If Beverly had any reservations, it was toward Steven's mother.

Just then she overheard a woman crying in the stall that was next to her.

"It's okay, Robin. We all have breakdowns sometimes. You'll get married one day, you'll see."

"I know, but when will it be my turn?" Robin wailed. "My eggs aren't getting any younger."

Beverly rolled her eyes at the conversation between her two best friends and contemplated lending an ear. She met her reflection in the mirror and took a good hard look. Screw it, she thought and walked out of the bathroom.

When she exited the ladies' room, low and behold, Parker stood there waiting for her with a beer.

"Everything all right?" he asked.

"Yeah, let's get out of here."

CHAPTER 5

Sonny had watched with interest as they acted and reacted every scene over and over. Even when she thought that they had nailed it, the director would yell "cut" and have some suggestions on how they could make it better. It was really tedious work, more so than she would have ever thought.

Lillian Grace, the actress who played the part of Beverly Litchfield, was absolutely beautiful. She had long luscious hair and flawless, glowing skin, with the help of a make-up artist, of course.

Sonny sat out of the way, writing in a note pad.

"Working on your next book?"

She looked up at Lillian and Dax, who were standing close by. "Oh, hi," she said, taken off guard.

"Dax said you were a writer."

Sonny looked at him curiously. "He did?"

"Yes, I would love to get a copy of your book."

"Well, right now, I'm still trying to get it published."

"I'm sure that Dax can help pull some strings for you." Lillian looked at him with a light in her eyes.

Oh, boy, Sonny thought, *the next Hollywood romance*. She wondered how Zola would feel about this.

"Isn't he so talented?" Lillian asked.

"Yes, it would seem he is," Sonny said. "In more ways than one."

Dax cleared his throat. "They called a wrap for the day," he said.

"Oh, I must have been preoccupied. I didn't notice. Your scenes today were really entertaining."

He stared at her seriously. "You think so?"

"I do."

"It was a pleasure to meet you, Sonny. I better get some beauty sleep. I can't have this hunk looking better than me," Lillian said.

"You're truly gorgeous, even more stunning in person," Sonny said kindly.

"You're too nice. Dax, she's good. I wish my assistant was that complimentary," Lillian said.

"She is good. I know it," Dax replied.

Sonny felt a blush creep across her face.

"I will see you all tomorrow."

Sonny watched as Lillian's perfect backside swayed rhythmically from side to side as she walked away. "Are you ready?" she asked.

"Yes, I just need to wash off this stage make up."

"Oh, I didn't realize that a hunk of a man needed make up."

"Shut up," he said playfully.

"I'll get the car."

ఌఌ

Sonny was waiting when Dax got to the car. He opened the back seat to throw his duffel bag in and saw the bouquet of dead flowers on the floor board.

"What the hell are these? What kind of guys are you dating?"

"Oh, those. I was going to tell you about that."

"What do you mean you were going to tell me? Tell me what?"

"Read the card and take note of the ribbon that's interlaced amongst the lovely dead petals," Sonny said as she pulled out of the set.

"'Any friend of Parker Maxwell is not a friend of mine. I pick them off one by one like dead decaying flowers on a vine.'" Dax sat in silence for a moment deep in thought. "What the hell?" he said finally.

"That's basically the same reaction my roommate had," Sonny said.

"Where and when did you find these?" Dax asked, bewildered.

"They were left in the downstairs lobby of my apartment by my mailbox. The strange part is that I was in and out last, night carrying in boxes for Hudson, and I know that they were not there at that time. Then we ordered pizza, and when he went down to pay the delivery guy, they were there. So it seems as if the sender knew when I would be home and waited for the opportune time to drop them off. I'm most concerned that he or she was watching me. It's a little unsettling, and did you notice the use of your new character's name, Parker Maxwell?"

"Yes, I noticed," Dax said quietly.

"Well, don't you think it's odd, considering the two messages you received directed toward Daniel Sampson? And don't you dare say that I'm reading too much into it. I don't know what kind of fan mail you're used to, but the only thing I'm used to getting in the mail is bills. And I'm not an expert on the subject, but doesn't it remind you of a funeral arrangement?"

"I was not going to say anything about you reading anything into it, Sonny. You have every right to be disgusted and scared. I never wanted this kind of attention to be reflected on anyone else around me. I'm sorry that you had to go through this," he said earnestly.

Sonny was slightly surprised by his serious reaction, and she was at a loss for words.

"What do you do want to do about it? Are you still interested in working for me? I understand if you want to remove yourself from the situation."

"Still work for you? Yes, it isn't your fault that some creep is trying to scare you and those around you. I just want to make sure that we're playing it safe and not underestimating what this person is capable of. I would also like to know what is motivating his or her obvious anger toward you. Is it a role you played or you personally? I mean, why use your aliases, and not just call you out directly?"

"I'm not sure of the answer to any of those questions, but I wish I knew. It was one thing when they got into my car or followed me to take a close up picture. Anyone can be sneaky enough to do that, and *Sampson's Soldiers* had already hit theaters, but to know enough to know that you're my new assistant and where you live, not to mention the role I have only just begun shooting takes some research. I could kill the bastard for going to your home."

"I admit I was pretty shaken up last night but, luckily, Hudson moved in early, so I wasn't alone. I still didn't get much sleep, but I'm naive on the normal protocol on how much good and bad attention you must get as an actor. I'm sure many people obsess about your life or think they know you when they really don't."

"All of that's true. Fortunately, most of my encounters are pleasant ones. This is new terrain for me as well. I've not exactly been on the Hollywood scene all that long. I'm truly sorry you were scared, though."

"Thank you, Dax. Just try to quit pissing people off, would ya?"

"You surprise the hell out of me," Dax said seriously.

"Why do you say that?" Sonny asked.

"Most women I know would be running for the hills, or at the very least demanding an armed escort. But you, you just confront it with your normal quick wit and logical sensibility. Why didn't you tell me about it this morning?"

Sonny gave him an arched eyebrow. "Really? When you slept through your alarm, and I had to basically dress you..." She trailed off remembering the way he had nuzzled and kissed her. She did not bring that part up. "And then when we were in the car, you were concentrating so hard on rehearsing your lines that I did not want to disturb you. It was your first day, and I wanted it to be a good one. I didn't want this to be a cause for distraction."

She pulled into the parking space assigned to him and put the car in park. When she turned to face him, he was staring at her intently with a piercing gaze. His dark eyes had grown even darker with his thoughts and almost blended in with the inky blackness of the night.

"You look pensive. Are you pensive?" she asked, trying to lighten the mood.

"I was just thinking that I was already distracted today."

"Really? Why? It did not come across in your performance. Did the first two messages get to you that much? Or maybe you're missing Zola?"

Dax silenced her by grabbing her face abruptly and covering her lips with his. She remained still, taken by surprise, but he palmed the sides of her face and let his fingers spread through her hair. His mouth was gentle as he parted her lips and slowly let his tongue enter her mouth.

It felt good and tasted good, too, but she pushed him away before it could go further.

"I was distracted today, thinking about this morning's kiss. And I couldn't wait to try it again," he whispered.

Heat flamed to her cheeks along with other places, and she was glad that he could not see the other places as well. She also hoped the darkness masked the mad blush that had taken over her face. "Dax, I understood this morning that you were half asleep and thought I was someone else. Your girlfriend is out of town, and we have been and will be spending a lot of time together, so I'm probably the most convenient option, but we both know you have plenty of other options," Sonny said. "So maybe you should take one of them up on it, or better yet, don't, if you want to make your relationship with Zola work. But I work for you, so this cannot happen. I understand your previous assistant, Rachel, succumbed to the charm that's Daxton Knight, but ultimately she doesn't have a job because of it. I need this job, and, besides, it just isn't a good idea."

"You're right, it probably isn't," he said.

"Okay then," she said with a shaky breath. "But we're good, I still have a job?"

"What kind of person do you think I am? I'm not paying for you to be my call girl. Yes, of course, you still have a job. I made a move based on a whim, you shot me down. I can handle it," Dax replied easily.

"Okay then. I'll heat you up some dinner and call it a night."

"I'm really not an invalid, as much as you may think I am."

"I know that, but please let me do it. I don't want to end the day on a sour note."

"Suit yourself. But nobody's sour here. I can respect your stance."

Sonny warmed him up a plate of leftovers, watered the plants, and set his alarm. "Now, no turning it off in the morning."

"I'll try not to."

She was about to leave when he said, "Who's Hudson? I didn't know you had a roommate. Or does he not have his own room?"

"He has his own room." Sonny wrinkled her nose at him. "That would be awkward if he didn't, considering I just met him. Hudson Law is his name, and he's a writer-slash-artist that was moving out of an ex-girlfriend's place. He's helping with the rent."

"Hmm."

"What does that noise mean?" Sonny asked.

"What noise?"

"That sarcastic little sound that you just made when I was talking about Hudson."

"Nothing, it's just that a man fresh out of a relationship will be on the hunt and living in that close of quarters—just be careful, that's all I'm saying."

"Pretty sound advice, coming from you," she mused.

"Okay, I guess I deserve that for crossing the line. But call what I did a kind of experiment. I had a hypothesis, I performed the experiment, there were factors that were out of my control, but I got the results."

"Okay, Mr. Metaphor, I have been referred to as an experiment and a potential rebound. I'm going to pick my ego up off of the floor, and go home where we can sulk and eat chocolate together."

Dax laughed. "That's not what I meant, I hope I did not offend you."

"Lucky for you, I try to not be easily offended, but that charm you think you have all figured out, you may want to work on that. See you in the AM."

When she was out the door, he said, "Sonny, don't you want to know the results of my hypothesis? I was right."

"I'm afraid to ask. Maybe you'll tell me some other time."

"Will do."

"Oh, and, Dax, I thought about giving the flowers to Miles, the forensic pathologist, who is married to my friend Vivian. Maybe he could test it for prints, or do whatever it is they do. You never know. It could prove beneficial."

"I think that's a good idea. And, Sonny, thanks."

"For what?"

"For having courage and not walking away."

She smiled. "You're welcome."

ଔଔ

Sonny got back to her car and used the key fob to unlock the doors. Once inside, she relocked them just for safety measures and glanced at the floor board to look at the flowers.

She gasped and quickly picked up the phone to call Dax.

He answered on the first ring. "Change your mind?"

"No, Dax, the bouquet, it's gone."

CHAPTER 6

Beverly only felt mildly guilty for allowing Parker to sneak her out of her own bachelorette party. Her friends were so snickered, they wouldn't even notice. She had given the bartender strict instructions to have a cab waiting for them when it was the last call for alcohol.

Beverly could not really say why she had agreed to hang out with Parker Maxwell other than that she had felt like she was being suffocated. She could not breathe and had been struggling for air for quite some time. Meanwhile, all of the wedding planning was like a noose getting tighter and tighter.

She had not expected to feel this way when Steven had proposed. She had thought he was exactly what she wanted. And in many ways, he was. It was the obvious next step in their relationship, and they already lived together, unofficially, of course, so as not to upset his mother. So what was she afraid of?

Beverly found herself rationalizing out loud and trying in earnest to convince Parker that she was supposed to be with her fiancé. "He is smart, like incredibly smart."

"Of course he is, he proposed to you. I have to give the guy some credit," Parker said smoothly.

"I thought you said marriage was for dummies, hopeless romantics, and that men who proposed were saps."

"I still stand by what I said, but I suppose there are exceptions to every rule," he said genuinely.

"Are you calling me the exception?"

"Take it as you wish, but I hope that Steven knows how lucky he is that you said yes."

"Oh, you only feel that way because I brushed you off, and I'm unavailable. All men enjoy a good challenge. They like to remind themselves they can still conquer the female species. I would just be another one of your conquests, a notch on your belt, and then you would be saying that Steven's a poor sucker who's marrying a lying, adulterous bitch."

Parker pondered that thought. "Normally I would tend to agree with your very astute observation, but in this case, within five minutes I knew that you were none of those things."

"Oh, yeah, well what am I then?"

"You're beautiful, astoundingly perceptive, and intuitive. You're not full of yourself, but you carry a quiet confidence. You have a slow-and-steady-wins-the-race mentality, but you long to know what it feels like to fly by the seat of your pants. You're feeling lost, and since you're always self-assured, this has you questioning things even more, and, most importantly—now, listen close because my true compliments are few and far between." Parker leaned in to whisper, "You're are a smartass."

She stared at him slightly open mouthed, pretending to be appalled.

"What, did I hit the nail on the head?" Parker asked.

"I am so not a smart ass, Mr. Stalker," she said sarcastically.

They walked in silence for a few moments.

"Okay, in all seriousness. I have been feeling pretty stifled. It's just that Steven's mother is so overbearing and does everything for him. She's so over the top, but he will never go against her wishes. I truly believe that if it came down to it, he would choose to keep her happy over me. She loves order and accountability, planning and—"

Parker pretended to snore. "Sounds like a drag."

"My point exactly."

"I hope Steven did not inherit his mother's award winning personality."

"No, not at all. Steven is caring, kind, funny—"

"He makes you laugh?" Parker asked suspiciously.

Beverly paused and stopped in the middle of the sidewalk to drink out of her brown paper bag.

"He's actually not that funny. Come to think of it, he doesn't get my jokes either. If somebody asked, I would say we laugh together, but truthfully I don't know that we do. And he isn't that kind either. Once, we walked past a homeless man, and instead of giving him money, which Steven has plenty of, he said, 'Here is a tip, get a job.' and kicked the can of change over. The man got up quickly to gather the change which only amounted to a couple of dollars. I stopped to help him pick it up, and the man's eyes were so wounded and ashamed. I tucked a twenty into his hand, and you would have thought it was raining Benjamins. 'Bless you, bless you,' he repeated over and over. I apologized profusely for Steven's behavior. Later, Steven blamed it on the alcohol he had consumed that night, but I don't believe he was truly sorry. I think he just recognized my disgust and worried I had a lesser opinion of him. I realize now that I did and I still do." Beverly sat down on the edge of the sidewalk and started breathing in quick short breaths. "I'm so scared that I have known him forever, but never really seen who he truly is."

She panted with anxiety. Parker sat next to her and faced her toward him.

"Hey, it's okay, breathe. You don't have to figure it out this instant. You're a smart woman. You'll know what you need to do when the time comes. Right now, just relax and breathe."

He coached her, as they took deep breaths together.

When her breathing had slowed, he said, "There you go. That's it. Welcome back."

She rested her head on his shoulder as he wrapped an arm around her. It was so comforting and warm. The chill in the air, combined with the alcohol, had Parker's embrace feeling oh so inviting. She abruptly lifted her head. "Stop."

"What did I do wrong?" he asked.

"Nothing, that's the problem. Don't pretend to be nice to me. Don't take advantage of my vulnerabilities."

"Beverly, I have no intention of doing that. I'm just enjoying spending time with you."

"But we shouldn't be doing that. I'm an almost-married woman."

"Okay, I take it back. I hate spending time with you."

Beverly laughed and slapped his arm playfully. "Seriously, you're a man. Would you let your mother dictate your every move?"

"I guess my answer would have to be no. My mother left before I hit double digits. The summer before my tenth birthday. I was left with my stepfather who made no secret that he was none too happy about it."

"Oh, I'm so sorry, Parker. Is that why you have such a bitter opinion of marriage and happily ever after? It must have been hard growing up without a maternal figure at such an impressionable age."

She raised her hand up to brush away his hair off his forehead, and he grabbed her wrist gently. For a second, neither of them moved, lost in the moment, wondering if they would ever get another one.

Suddenly, Parker was pulled away from her by the back of his shirt, and a fist slammed into his nose.

"What the hell are you doing with my fiancé? Are you trying to rob her, you little punk?"

"Steven, no!" she screamed.

One of the groomsmen held Parker beneath his arms so that Steven could take another sucker punch. Beverly jumped onto Steven's back.

"Stop, Steven, he's not a bad guy. He was helping me."

∽∽

Sonny watched as Dax was sucker punched repeatedly, and fake blood dripped down his face soaking his shirt. He had to change the shirt a few times when it had gotten too bloody to be realistic.

Finally, the director must have gotten what he wanted because he called a wrap for the day.

"You did amazing today," Lillian said sweetly. "Keep up the good work, and we'll be ahead of schedule."

"I'm only as good as my costar. So you must be amazing enough to make both of us look good."

"Oh, Dax, you're too much. Will I see you at Landry's Saturday night?"

"I'm not sure yet. It was kind of going to depend on…Well, I have to check my schedule," he amended.

"Let me guess, it was going to depend on if Zola comes to town. You think I don't hear the latest gossip? Bring her—the more, the merrier. I hear the filet mignon is to die for."

"Well, Zola's a vegetarian, but I'll try to make an appearance."

"Please do," Lillian said. "Oh, and Sonny, you're more than welcome to join us. We would love to have you."

"U—Um," Sonny stuttered. She wasn't sure about the protocol for social gatherings, but she was sure that Dax didn't want her to tag along as his date.

"A lot can happen in two days. I'll let you know," she said brightly.

"Great. See you guys tomorrow." Lillian shook her ass as she walked away.

"She totally wants you," Sonny said.

"Really? I think that's just how she is to everyone."

"Hmm, well she's gorgeous, and I'm sure you love acting alongside her every day."

"Yeah, she's very talented," he said, distracted.

"What is it, Dax?

"Nothing. Come help me scrub this blood off of my face."

Twenty minutes later, when Dax's face was good and raw and the sink was stained red, he finally felt clean.

"I think you might have really made me bleed," he said, touching his sensitive face.

She laughed as she gathered the washcloths. "Oh, waah, you're such a baby." Out of the corner of her eye, she spotted an envelope, and the red letters scrawled to look like blood caused her stomach to do flip-flops. "Dax, I think we have another message."

His head whipped around, and his gaze landed at where she stared at the envelope. He crossed over to it quickly and saw that it was addressed to both Dax and Sonny. He pulled out a picture. It was of them from the previous night when Dax had kissed her in the car.

The message below it read:

Dax and Sonny sitting in a tree, K-I-S-S-I-N-G. There is more where this came from, and when I am through with you, it won't be fake blood pouring from your nose.

Sonny's hand flew to her mouth. "Dax, why is this happening? This picture cannot get out. What are we going to do?"

Dax had a grim look on his face. "We're going to have to do something, and that's what I was trying to avoid—alert the authorities. I was really hoping to not make headlines and give this creep what he or she wants—to be put in the spot light while humiliating me. But we can't risk it. I won't risk your safety."

"Maybe I can talk to Miles and see if he has some suggestions."

"In the meantime, I'm dropping you off at home, instead of the other way around. I don't want you to have to walk back down to your car in the dark alone," Dax said.

On the ride home, they were abnormally quiet with the exception of Sonny giving him directions.

"So, is your roommate going to be home?"

"Probably."

"That's good."

"Yeah, I guess," Sonny said. "So is Zola coming in to town this weekend?"

"Talking about a short trip on Saturday," Dax said.

"Oh, I bet you are excited."

"Sonny?"

"Yes."

"Don't worry about the pictures. I'm not. It's no big deal. Pictures always look worse than they actually are. Everyone knows that, especially in this industry."

"Unfortunately, I'm not in the industry, so I do not know what people will think."

"Sonny, you sound scared."

"Maybe I am. A little," she said meekly.

"Don't give this scumbag the benefit of knowing that he's getting to us."

"Easy for you to say."

When Dax pulled up in front of her apartment, he said, "Should I walk you up?"

"No, it's okay. She rolled her eyes. "Wouldn't want the paparazzi getting the wrong impression."

As far as he knew they had not been followed. "I don't care what people think," he said and grabbed her face with such force she lost her breath as his mouth greedily claimed hers.

There was an urgency from Dax that he had kept in control until now. Her mouth betrayed her as her lips parted and their tongues intertwined. She gasped, and his hands grabbed her hair in frenzied movement.

He spoke her name. "Sonny." Her pulse quickened, but after a moment he pulled away. "You should go up. I'll watch you to make sure you get there safely."

"You've got to stop doing that," she said breathlessly.

"Oh, you like it," he teased.

As she walked up the stairs to her building, she admitted to herself that maybe she rather did.

CHAPTER 7

Sonny was relieved to hear the television set when she put the key in the lock. She was pleased that Hudson was home and that she would not be alone. She would never have gotten any sleep otherwise because her paranoia would have devoured her.

It was an odd feeling to suddenly rely on someone that, by all accounts, she barely knew. When she opened the door, she was greeted by cheers so loud that it took a moment for her to realize that they were happy sounds and not a sign that she should duck for cover.

When Hudson saw her, he quieted down. "Oh, I'm sorry. I didn't hear you come in. I hope you don't mind, I invited Nathaniel over to watch the Cardinal versus Cubs game."

"Of course not, it's your house too. You can have people over whenever you like. I'm not your guardian.

You don't have to ask permission." She smiled. "Hell, I won't even give you a curfew."

Hudson laughed. "Well, in that case, Nate this is Sonny. Sonny this is Nate. Nate's new to the area. He's in town for some business. He's in the creative writing business too."

"Well, attempting to be," Nate chimed in. "I can't quite quit my day job yet. It's nice to meet you." He stuck out his hand and Sonny accepted.

"What brings you to town?" she asked.

"Pharmaceutical sales. We had a conference up near Chicago, but I have some family close by that would be mighty angry if I was this close to them and didn't re-route to come see them. That being said, there's a reason we only see each other a couple of times a year. I escaped to the coffee shop."

"Where I had to school him on who was the better baseball team," Hudson finished.

The cardinals were up six to nothing going into the bottom of the third, and the Cubs had just struck out, while Nate grimaced. "They're making me look bad, but we all know Cubs' fans are as loyal as they come. I'm not a fair-weather fan. One day, the curse will be broken, and we will reign again."

"Oh, please." Hudson rolled his eyes. "Let the world championships speak for themselves. Count them on your fingers—oh wait, that's right, you're one short."

"We'll see who's standing on the field come October. It's early days yet. What do you think Sonny?" Nate asked her.

"Well, clearly you two have more time on our hands than me, but they don't call it Red October for nothing. We Cards' fans are no strangers to the playoffs, and the lineup is looking good this year."

"Oh, be still my heart, a woman who knows baseball. It's too bad you root for the enemy."

Sonny laughed. "You're talking to the woman whose Grandpa was a season ticket holder and doted on his favorite granddaughter. I spent many a day with that man, listening to the infamous Jack Buck announce play by play across the radio of my granddad's beat up pickup truck. He didn't spend money on much, but there was no expense spared when it came to his team. He even played in the minors but settled into farm life before he ever got called up. So you'll never convert me."

"Oh, it's just as well. Like I said, you have to admire loyalty."

"That's right," Sonny agreed.

"Are you just getting home from work?" Hudson asked.

She sighed. "Yes."

"Long day on the set, huh?"

"You could say that."

"Set? You make movies?" Nate asked.

"Oh, good Lord, no," she said. "I wouldn't know the first thing. I prefer to write. Now, I wouldn't complain if one of my books became a movie," she joked. "No, I'm a temporary assistant to Daxton Knight."

"The actor? Hmm, that must be interesting. Does he really have the life or what?"

"I would say yes. The man has a life of luxury and couldn't be on time if his life depended on it, but I can't say that he doesn't work hard. There's a lot more that goes into making a scene than I would have ever imagined."

"I'm sure there is. Why the temporary position?"

"I'm just filling in while he is in town shooting his new movie, making a little extra cash. Ideally, I'll write full time someday, hopefully sooner rather than later."

"Cheers to that." The men clicked their beers together and tilted them up to take a swig.

"Sonny, would you like one?" Hudson asked.

"No, thank you. I think I deserve a long hot bath after my day."

"Okay, we'll try to keep it down out here."

"Honestly, I'm so tired, it probably wouldn't even matter. I want you to feel at home here."

She squeezed his bicep, and he smiled appreciatively.

Sonny was on her way down the hall when Nate said, "By the way, Sonny, I didn't think you directed a movie, I assumed you were staring in one."

ଓଃଓଃ

The world must be coming to an end, Sonny thought as she sank beneath the bubbles. It wasn't as if she had never been hit on before, but never had she had a plethora of men surrounding her.

First and foremost, a movie star had kissed her and not just an innocent kiss either. Then she found herself living with a man that she was still getting to know and that roommate's friend openly flirted with her, although an innocent enough comment was still a flirtation nonetheless. She had never felt like a hot commodity, but she was in uncharted waters. It was for the best to ignore them all, she decided.

Sonny had bigger fish to fry rather than worry about some play boys whose advances wouldn't amount to anything. She could return friendly banter with the best of them but tended to shy away from making any bold moves.

No, she had a book to get published, a second one dancing in her head, waiting to be put down on paper, a paycheck to collect, and a stalker by association to decamp from. She would say her plate was full, and she was choking on it now without asking for seconds.

Still, she was flattered, to say the least. She was cute enough, in the kind of way that would make a good wife someday, but she wouldn't describe herself as irresistibly sexy. Not in the dirty, worth-it-to-have-the-affair, mistress kind of way. She was pretty but was more known for being the pretty girl's friend, and she had played the role her whole life. She liked to read and to write, and pretty girls were much too busy going on dates to do either.

Sonny was a feminist and believed in equality and all that it entailed. That didn't change the fact that sexy girls like Zola dated the movie stars, while she was an assistant to one. She only shared sparks with him out of close proximity, easy opportunity, and…for lack of a better term…to pass the time.

But Dax wasn't the only one in close proximity. There was a not-so-amicable fan that did not view him or her, guilty by association, so favorably. The question was why?

Had Dax flirted with the wrong woman or not taken the time to sign an autograph, or was it more than that? Was this unidentified messenger just trying to keep them in a heightened state of alarm, or was his plan more terrifying than that? Did he plan to attempt to carry out some of his anonymous threats? Obviously, his bluffs were atrocious enough, but she hoped he didn't plan on putting any action behind his words. The part that left her feeling more anxious was how he seemed to be a hair breath's away.

He and his camera lens were able to capture Dax close at hand, although, of course, the actor wouldn't have noticed because he was used to the flash of a camera everywhere he went. However, the secret sender was also aware of what scenes Dax had been filming and used that to his advantage.

Sonny felt chill bumps go up her arms, regardless of the steamy temperatures of her bath water. She glanced at the time and knew she should call it a night in order to appear presentable in the morning. She sank beneath the foam and held her breath to allow the calming Zen of the water to absorb her fragile nerves.

Suddenly, a commotion from somewhere close by had her quickly coming up for air.

Hudson yelled her name, and she yelped with startled surprise. He turned his back impulsively.

"Sorry, oh God, I'm so sorry. It was foolish of me to barge in here, but I called your name out a couple of times to say good night and, when you didn't answer, I thought the worst. Then when I came in here, you were submerged under the water, and I panicked."

Sonny grabbed a towel to cover her nakedness and tried to steady her racing heart.

"Are you okay? I'm sorry for intruding."

"I'm okay. I'm just not used to living along side of a member of the opposite sex," she managed to say.

"I guess I'm not the best at this either," he said sheepishly over his shoulder. "Can we pretend like this awkward scenario never happened?"

"Agreed," Sonny said.

"Sorry again," Hudson apologized profusely.

"N—No, I, uh—" she stuttered. "As awkward as this was, I guess I appreciate you being concerned."

"When I saw you, I was afraid that it was a Whitney Houston situation. I've got to calm my imagination but, on that note, I'm going to bed. I guess I'll see you in the morning."

Sonny clutched the towel firmly to her breasts. "Yeah, I'll see you then."

When Hudson left, she let out a breath and quickly stepped out of the tub to dress. What a day this had turned out to be. When she was safely within the confines of her queen sized bed, she set the alarm and lay back on her pillow. Knowing that sleep would not come, no matter how much she longed for sweet dreams to overtake her subconscious and engulf her in sandy beaches and sunny blue skies, she uncapped her pen and opened a notebook.

There once was an inspired writer who longed for nothing more than to chase her dreams. That all changed when she was propelled into an unknown world of fame and notoriety. It was a supposedly amazing opportunity of working with a well-known actor that caused her existence to never be the same. For better or worse was yet to be determined.

ഗദ

When Sonny awakened, her eyes were grainy, and

her body yearned to roll over and pull the pillow back over her head. Her brain was not prepared to be awake and screamed at her in angry opposition with a pounding headache.

She had, against her better judgment, written into the wee hours of the morning. She only called it quits when her hand was so sore that she was sure it would fall off and, even then, she had drifted to sleep with her notebook in hand and her pen slipping to her side mid-sentence. She was aggravated with herself now, but when inspiration struck, who was she to deny it? It was better than suffering from writer's block.

Although the impending migraine sure said differently. Unfortunately, she could not allow herself the leisure of pressing snooze and being lackadaisical by lying in bed amongst her down pillows because her boss was no stranger to the guilty pleasure himself. She needed to ensure that she arrived fifteen minutes early to drag his cute self-indulgent ass out of bed so that he could gripe and complain enough to get it out of his system before he had to appear charming and proficient on set.

Sonny threw back the covers and went about her morning routine, making sure to apply extra concealer to hide her tired eyes. She was dressed in one of her favorite outfits with worn and comfortable jeans. She assumed that the dress code she had previously adhered to held no relevance as it was pretty casual on set amongst all the people behind the camera. She straightened and then curled her hair, only to brush it out again. Why was she so indecisive today? she wondered as she applied a pale pink lip gloss to her lips and debated on dangly earrings or studs.

Was she really being this girl? She wanted to roll her eyes at her reflection in the mirror. She refused to admit the reasoning behind her careful consideration of her outfit. Dax worked alongside Lillian Grace, a beautiful and voluptuous actress whose heart appeared to be as big as the breasts that covered it. He dated Zola Wallace and, although he revealed very little about their relationship, what was not to like? She was outwardly gorgeous and the come-screw-me look she was notorious for, along with her luscious pout, could persuade even the most frugal consumer to purchase the product that she was getting paid to sell. She was a walking advertisement for sex, and Sonny was a behind-the-scenes yellow pages' advertisement for snuggling.

What did she really expect? She expected to not be so delusional and be a little more confident than this.

"Geez, Sonny, pull yourself together. Do not let this lifestyle get the better of you. You're the next in-demand author who is about to have your book sold out in stores. You are capable, strong, and gifted. You are not in competition, you run your own race—"

"And you are in first place, girl."

Sonny jerked away from the mirror, embarrassed at having been caught in her private pep talk.

Hudson stood there smiling, humor twinkling in his eyes. “Sorry, did I catch you off guard again? I certainly did not mean to.”

“No, I’m just mortified, I confess.”

“Please, don’t be. I enjoyed listening to your speech. You’re all of those things, at least since I’ve known you. Do you want to talk about what has got you worked up?”

“Where do I begin? It’s too long to start now, but I appreciate your willingness to lend an ear.”

“I’m here anytime. What are roommates for?” Hudson handed her a cup of green tea with a lemon wedge.

“Bless you,” Sonny said. “I’ve got to run, but thanks a million.”

“Sonny, whatever it is, don’t doubt yourself. Stand tall with pride because you have a lot of amazing qualities that many others long to have.”

“Thanks, Hud. You’re getting good at this roommate thing.”

“Does it make up for walking in on you naked last night?”

“Almost,” she said as she walked out the door with her head held high, exuding a confidence that she would channel from his kind words. Her disposition had turned from faintly sour to sweet.

CHAPTER 8

When she arrived at Dax's apartment, she decided she would not bring up the kiss. She would do her best to appear indifferent, unshakeable, and in control, but her guard would be up in case he decided to succumb to any more shenanigans.

She knocked lightly on the door, key in hand, and was surprised to find it open. Oh, goodness, the world really was coming to an end, could it be that the world famous Daxton Knight had awoken on time?

Sonny entered the foyer and softly said. "Hello?"

She couldn't be sure that this less-than-humble man wasn't parading around naked or, worse, admiring his fit physique in a mirror somewhere. Sonny was about to call out to him when she heard voices coming from a distance. *That's weird, who would he be talking to at this early hour?* She followed the voices and stopped short of the bedroom door, when she heard a female's voice.

"I just wanted to surprise you a day early, lover."

"I'm surprised, that's for sure," Dax said.

"Isn't it a nice surprise? You don't sound very excited to see me." Zola's voice held a pout.

"I'm very happy to see you. It was very thoughtful of you to arrive early. It's just that I'm usually running late in the mornings, and it drives my assistant crazy. I was actually attempting to be on time for once."

"Well, boo, I thought we would have time for a morning wake up call."

"That sounds enticing, it really does, but unfortunately, I have to be on set early today."

"Aren't you the lead role? It is not like they are going to start without you."

Dax sighed. "No, but I have a good repertoire with all of the cast and crew. I don't want to start giving them a reason to think I'm a diva or above their rules. Besides, Sonny will be here shortly to pick me up."

"But you're a little bit above the rules, Daxton. The movie wouldn't amount to anything if you weren't in it. And who works for who? That girl is your employee. If you tell her to wait, she waits."

"While I appreciate your vote of confidence, the script is a good one and I'm lucky to be asked to be a part of it, and Sonny does not work like that. She does her best to keep me in line."

"I'm sure she does, just like Rachel tried to, but aren't you above their pay grade, Dax?" she asked angrily.

"It isn't even like that, Zola. You're being paranoid for nothing. Sonny's just a no-namer waitress, who wants to be a writer someday. I'm letting her ride on my coat tails until this job is over. She came on the recommendation of a friend of a friend. I'm just being a nice guy helping out a charity case."

"So do you or don't you find her attractive?" Zola asked pointedly.

"I mean I would be lying if I said she wasn't all right, but nothing compared to you, babe."

"Of course she isn't." Zola's smile was evident in her voice. "I'm just making sure you still have your priorities straight. Don't get caught up with no-namers. We're going places Daxton, and you don't want to be pulled down."

Sonny's face burned with anger and embarrassment and tears flooded her eyes. Zola was a bitch, but Dax's words had cut deep. How dare he insinuate that she needed him? Who did he think he was? She wasn't riding anyone's coat tails, and it was her who was being inconvenienced by his stalker.

Her fury and humiliation were mounting as Dax and Zola entered the kitchen. She wanted to run away, but pride had made her stand steady. She quickly opened the refrigerator to appear busy and not as if she had been eaves dropping.

From behind the door of the fridge, she tried to quickly wipe away her tears before they were noticed.

"Sonny," Dax said. "How long have you been here?"

She slowly closed the one barrier saving her from facing him. "I just got here. I thought I would grab some waters for the road. Hello, Ms. Wallace." She redirected her attention to Zola. "Will you be joining us on set today?"

"Oh, I planned to go shopping later, but I guess I could spend my morning watching you work," Zola answered to Dax.

"Well then, we better get going." Sonny power walked to the door, and Dax followed.

One look at her face, and he knew she had heard everything.

"Sonny, wait. Can I talk to you privately?"

"Save it, Dax," she muttered so that his girlfriend couldn't hear. "I wouldn't want to waste any of your precious time."

"Oh, someone must have gotten their feelings hurt," Zola smirked.

The two of them, Sonny and Dax, rode in silence with Zola occasionally breaking the tension with melodramatic questions about the area. Sonny remained quiet and left it to Dax to make mundane conversation. He tried to meet Sonny's eyes in the rearview mirror, but she refused to be pulled in his direction, focusing only on the road. Her hands gripped the steering wheel so tight her knuckles were white, and he noticed one lone tear drop stuck on her lashes.

She pulled in the assigned space with Dax's name on it and put the car in park. When Zola and Dax had exited the car, she rolled down the window. "I have some things to do today, so I'll be back to pick you up when it's time. You can text me when you're finished."

"You aren't staying?" Dax asked, alarmed. "What if I need you?"

"I doubt you will, and there are plenty of others that I'm sure would be of assistance to you."

Dax stared into her face, wishing he could see her eyes beneath her sunglasses and willing her to take them off.

"Look, honey, I don't know what Daxton lets you get by with, but you work for him, and this is his car. I mean seriously, Daxton. Where do you find these girls?"

"Zola." Dax held up a hand. "Would you do me a favor and get me more water from my trailer?"

Zola roller her eyes indignantly but made her way to his labeled lair. When Dax turned back toward Sonny, she was out of the car and pulling a key off of her keychain.

"Sonny, please. I'm not sure what you heard. I did not mean any of it."

"I heard it all, Dax. Every word of it."

"I was just trying to avoid a nagging argument from Zola."

"Mission accomplished," Sonny said.

"I know that you have every right to be angry. I said some hurtful things, but—"

"Why do you care what this no-name waitress, coat-tail riding, average-looking, charity case thinks?" Sonny asked with her voice cracking.

Dax winced at hearing his words replayed for him. "Sonny—"

"I said, save it, Dax. I'll let you get back to your life of going places, I certainly would not want to drag you down."

"You don't drag me down. Sonny, this is not how I wanted this to go."

He ran his hands through his hair. Sonny grabbed one of them and pressed the key into his palm.

"What is this?"

"It's the key to your apartment. I'm leaving the car here. I'm sorry for the short notice, but today was my last day."

She turned on her heel, and he called out after her, "Sonny, wait."

She continued marching purposefully away, and Zola handed him a water.

"Let her go. Girls like that are a dime a dozen."

Dax stared after her, as Sonny walked away. For someone who lived his life to please only himself, his conscience had finally found its voice.

CHAPTER 9

Sonny walked at a pace that was virtually a slow run, and if she could have run without making more of a spectacle out of herself, she would have.

"Sonny, why the rush?" a voice called out to her.

She was tempted to ignore it, but her manners got the best of her. She turned to see Lillian Grace waiting for her.

"Oh, hello, Lillian. I, um, just had some errands to get done today," Sonny said lamely, trying to keep the emotion out of her voice.

"You're in an awful hurry, so I won't keep you. But I was just wondering if you will be joining us for dinner tonight?"

"Oh, I don't believe so. I appreciate the invite, but I just don't think I can make it."

"That's a shame. I was really hoping to get everyone together. I know that the people behind the camera are just as important as the ones in front of it."

It took everything in Sonny's power to not snort with distain. The irony was almost too much to handle. Lillian was perceptive enough to catch the flicker of resentment that had crossed over her face.

"Uh, oh, trouble in paradise?"

"Paradise?" Sonny repeated.

"What did Dax do? Did his head get to big to fit through his shirt?"

"What makes you say that?" Sonny asked.

"Well, he is a man, after all. He was bound to say something stupid and most likely something he didn't mean. You seem pretty upset and aren't staying on set today while his model girlfriend is happily warming your chair, so one could conclude..."

Sonny didn't meet her knowing gaze and instead looked at her feet.

"Listen, Sonny, I don't pretend to know what transpired between the two of you, but I know what he has said about you to me, and all of it was good. He could not talk you up enough. The media may make it seem like we're above it all and that our opinions matter more than others, but at the end of the day, we're only human. We make mistakes just like everyone else. I know Dax thinks very highly of you, and I would hate to see your relationship ruined because of something he said or did."

"All I'll say is that I'm fairly certain that he meant every word, but it has been very nice getting to know you and a privilege watching you work. I look forward to seeing the end result in theaters."

"Oh, honey, you don't have to feed my ego. I hope you know I'm more down-to-earth than that. I really hope that I see you sooner. Besides, I look forward to reading that great book of yours. Maybe you'll remember me when it comes time to cast in a movie." Lillian gave her a hug. "Here, darling, I'm giving you my personal information. Maybe if you're feeling generous, you will send me your manuscript so that I can get an early start on it."

Sonny took the paper and stuffed it in her purse. "You are truly kind. Thank you." She started to walk away.

"Oh, and Sonny. I just want you to know, that I saw the way Dax looked at you. It did not go unnoticed."

Sonny looked back at her sullenly. "Well, it went unnoticed by me. He just isn't who I thought he was."

"Well, that's a shame." Lillian paused. "Because he said just the opposite about you. He said that you were better than he expected."

❧❧

"He was helping you do what?" Steven asked in an accusing voice.

"I was lost," Beverly said.

"Lost?" he asked skeptically.

"I got separated from my group of girlfriends. It would seem I had too much to drink." She chuckled nervously. "I couldn't seem to find my way as easily as I thought I could." Beverly stumbled a little on her heels for added effect. "This kind sir could see that I was highly intoxicated and was going to call me a cab." She turned to Parker as if it were her first time seeing the man clearly. "I appreciate your help. I apologize for the trouble. This is obviously my fiancé that I was rambling about, Steven. Steven, this is…I'm sorry, what was your name again?"

Beverly looked deeply at Parker, begging him with her eyes to play along.

"Garrett. My name is Garrett."

Beverly's smile only faltered for a moment. "Garrett, that's right. Well, I appreciate your help." She reached out her hand, and he slowly pulled his out of his pocket to shake hers gingerly.

"Look, no problem. I'm just glad you're going to be okay." Parker took a moment to look deep into her eyes before meeting Steven's menacing stare. "Look, no harm, pal. I'm glad you found her."

Steven looked back and forth between them cautiously. "Thank you for taking care of her. She is precious cargo, you know what I mean?"

Parker nodded his understanding as he dabbed at the corner of his lip.

"Hey, sorry about that, bud. You know how it must have looked, man to man."

Parker nodded again but said nothing.

"Well, you ready to go?" Steven asked Beverly, and without waiting for an answer, he looked back at Parker. "Thanks, Garrett, but I think I've got it from here."

Steven patted the man's shoulder and called for an Uber driver to pick them up. He grabbed Beverly's elbow to lead her away, and she risked looking back one last time as Parker stared at her meaningfully. As Steven's larger-than-life friends followed behind, one of them shoulder checked Parker while the other one snickered.

Parker watched the group walk away as he gritted his teeth. They were so not Beverly's type of people, and they most definitely weren't his either. He wasn't really a fan of the dumb jock bullies that never grew up past scoring the winning touchdown at the most important game of the season in high school. For some, that was the best they would ever be.

It was sad really, but Beverly had said that Steven was a very successful lawyer, and his family came from money.

No amount of money could buy you class or dignity. Beverly deserved better than those buffoons, but there was a good chance that he would never get the chance to tell her that.

He hadn't really believed in fate and surely not love at first sight, but yet it was a random encounter that brought him and Beverly together tonight. He would like to think that it was more than luck.

But now, she was walking away, and he had no idea if he would ever see her again. That thought made him want to hit something or someone, preferably someone by the name of Steven Calvird. The stupid prick had gotten him good, sucker punched him while his buddies prepared to hold him down. There was nothing Parker could do with it being three on one, and both Parker and Steven had known it.

The more he thought about it and felt his swollen lip throb in pain, the more angry he became. Who sucker punches someone in a jealous rage? Obviously, that same prick was smart enough to propose to Beverly. God, Parker hoped to hell she was smart enough to not go through with pledging herself to Steven forever and always, for better or worse. If she did, it was guaranteed to be worse, and Parker had already decided she deserved a man willing to always give his best.

He walked the streets for a long time, not wanting to go home. He might as well have been punched in the gut instead of his face, given the hollow feeling he felt in the pit of his stomach.

ഗദ

When the driver pulled up to pick up Beverly, he was driving a small, economy-sized car.

"It's going to be a tight squeeze, but I'm sure we can all fit," Beverly said.

"Oh, no, babe. I got the ride just for you."

"You aren't coming with me?" she asked, surprised.

"Sorry, Bev, but it's bachelor party night. We still have places and people to see," he said, nudging his best friends who readily agreed.

"But it's already so late."

"Maybe, but some of us can handle our alcohol, drunkey," he said teasingly. "Besides, it's probably a good thing you're going home now so that you will be ready to meet Mother tomorrow."

"Oh, yes, wouldn't want to disappoint Mother," she said sarcastically.

"What is that supposed to mean?" Steven asked.

"Nothing." She sighed. "I guess I'm just not feeling like myself."

"Go home and sleep it off."

Steven gave her a quick kiss and closed the door.

As the car pulled away with Beverly in it, she rolled down the window in time to hear him say, "Got rid of the old ball and chain, let's get this party started."

She rolled her eyes and thought back on the night. She could not believe that Steven had hit Parker. Well, yes, she actually could. He wasn't above resorting to physical violence or throwing a temper tantrum when he was angry, and Parker had been about to kiss her. Hadn't he? She was sure she had not imagined it, but Parker's persistence was surely due to her rejection of his advances. He would try harder to convince himself he could win her over, right?

But what was her excuse? She had been about to kiss him back, right? At the very least, Steven had interrupted a moment. He had intercepted her at just the right time. She wondered why Parker had faked his name."

Beverly opened her palm from which he had pressed the folded up business card when they shook hands before Steven led her away.

On it was a phone number. She felt a glimmer of hope. Beverly knew that she should throw it away immediately, but she could not force herself to do it.

She smiled down at the small cardboard piece of paper and placed it protectively in her pocket.

ಲಾಲ

When the final scene had been shot, Lillian asked Dax, "Where did Zola run off to?"

"She had plans to do some shopping," he muttered.

"Why so glum?" she asked.

"I'm just tired, I guess."

"It wouldn't have anything to do with Sonny, would it?"

Dax did not meet her knowing gaze. "No, why? Have you talked to her?"

"I saw her leaving in a hurry, and when I asked her about dinner, she said she wouldn't be able to make it. She seemed pretty upset. Did you two have a falling out?"

"I guess you could say that," he said.

"Come on, Dax, what did you do?"

"How do you know it was me?"

"I saw the way you looked at her and heard the way you spoke so highly of her, and then she just up and quit. I know what a woman with her feelings hurt looks like."

Dax sighed. "She overheard a conversation between Zola and me. It wasn't meant for her ears. I said some harsh things that I wish I could take back, but Zola was acting jealous, and I guess I was just attempting to placate her."

"So you screwed up?" Lillian said.

"Yeah, I guess I did," Dax admitted.

"So what are you going to do about it?"

"There is not much I can do. She left."

"Come on, Daxton. There is always something you can do to make it right. The world is full of second chances."

"Well, I'm not sure I deserve one. You didn't hear what was said."

"No, I did not, and I probably don't want to know. You would probably make me side with Sonny."

He smiled a faint grin. "Of course, you would. You women stick together."

"Except for Zola. She's not really a girl's girl."

"No, that she is not," Dax agreed.

"Maybe you need to reevaluate who you spend your time with."

Dax said nothing but took in Lillian's words.

"So I will ask again, what are you going to do about it?"

"What do you think I should do?" Dax asked.

"You could start by groveling and apologizing."

"I tried that. It was too soon."

"Well, in that case, you should give me Sonny's number," Lillian said matter-of-factly.

"Why? What are you going to do?"

"For starters, I'm going to get her to that dinner party."

CHAPTER 10

Sonny entered her apartment and was greeted with silence, with the exception of the welcoming click of Hudson's keyboard. She retreated to her desk and opened her laptop while going over the uncomfortable morning's events.

Her cheeks burned with embarrassment and hurt as Dax's words replayed in her mind. She felt like a fool for believing that this job opportunity could actually work out. She did not belong in their crowd. She was honestly too good for them because never in her life would she treat someone as low as they had made her feel.

She stared at the words she had written the night before and was tempted to delete everything she had let pour out of her, but, instead, she settled on crumbling up the paper that the first draft had been handwritten on. If she were going to continue the creation, then at least she had her villain of the story, she mused.

Her phone rang a few times, which she chose to ignore. She did not feel like talking at the moment. No, she was going to use this rejection as a spring board and delve deeper into her writing. Her hands flew across the keyboard as life circumstance intertwined with her art. At the very least, the emotions would be authentic.

The damsel in distress would not be the cowardly meek woman. She was going to grow through this situation and become the heroin. Then her own words struck her with irony. *Life imitates art*. Isn't that what Dax's stalker had said in his first message? Had Dax hurt someone else who held a grudge? Was someone angry enough that they planned to deliver threats and make him pay for his bad behavior? It wasn't any of her concern now, she guessed.

Maybe if there was a bright side to the situation, it was that Dax's stalker would get wind that she was no longer tied to him and leave her alone.

"Sonny, are you okay?"

Startled out of her deep thoughts, Sonny became aware of Hudson's presence and quickly wiped away the hot crocodile tears that had spilled down her cheeks.

"Oh, Hudson, I didn't see you standing there," Sonny said.

"I feel like I keep barging in on you at the worst times. You're home early. What's up?" he asked concerned.

Sonny hesitated only momentarily before she unleashed the day's events. "I quit my assistant job today. I just couldn't be around those people anymore. It wasn't really my scene."

"What do you mean? I thought it was going well."

"It was, or at least I thought it was, until his girlfriend, Zola the model, decided to arrive a day early. Apparently, she has a problem with me being in the picture, but I overheard Dax reassuring her. I don't hold a candle to her in the looks department, which I openly admit is true, but to hear the way they talked about it was rather humiliating. I'm just a waitress, who he let work for him as a charity case because I needed to ride his coat tails to get my book published."

"That arrogant bastard said that?" Hudson asked, feeling his anger mount for her.

"Yes, but what's worse is that I let that arrogant bastard kiss me, knowing it was wrong. I told him it was a bad idea the first time, but that didn't stop me from letting him do it again last night. And if that isn't bad enough, his stalker left him a picture of us in a compromising position, promising that there are more where that came from. So now I have to worry about being a part of a scandal of a salacious love triangle when I want nothing more than to be rid of them."

"Hold up, wait. A stalker, you said?"

Sonny was on such a rampage of verbal diarrhea that she did not realize he was staring at her in confusion. "Oh, yes, Dax has been getting some rather upsetting messages from an unknown person. It started right before he came here, but it seems the distance from California did not slow the messenger down, and he or she followed him here."

"Is that what the dead flowers were all about?"

"Yes, I guess his stalker realized I was in close connection to Daxton Knight the movie star and took it upon himself to find out where I lived."

"Sonny, this could be really dangerous."

"You're telling me. I think that Dax is really worried, but doesn't want to let on like it bothers him. Instead, he has taken the nonchalant approach, but the other night he insisted on driving me home, so I know that the seriousness of the threats has occurred to him."

"He should really take it more seriously. At least he had the common sense enough to worry about your safety. How many times has this person reached out, and are you sure it's the same person every time?"

"Yes, it has to be the same person. The threats all carry the same undertone of doom and gloom. Each message seems to be more intense. It started with a message written for his first character, Daniel Sampson and said '*Life imitates art.*' The message was found in the visor of Dax's personal car before he came here to start filming.

In the movie, Daniel Sampson was killed by a fellow soldier. The next threat I stumbled upon while sorting through some mail. It was written much like a ransom note with cut outs of letters from newspapers and magazines. It was also directed at Sampson, saying that he is never alone and that the writer could choose when he would meet his demise so he should spend his last days wisely. It was accompanied by a picture of him and his last assistant in a public setting. I think he was trying to let Dax know that he could get that close to him at any time without his knowledge, especially because so many people swarm Dax at any given time."

"Those are death threats," Hudson exclaimed.

"Yes, well he told me not to read too far into it. I think he was trying to avoid the media catching wind of it, and I understood, but then the flowers were delivered to my house, as you know, and the card read 'any friend of Parker Maxwell is not a friend of mine' and said they would 'pick them off one by one like dead flowers on a vine.' Parker is Dax's character in the movie he is shooting, *For Better or Worse*. I believe that after the person reached out to me, it made it that much more real for Dax. It showed him to what lengths they were willing to go. But it did not end there. Dax finished shooting a scene where he was bloodied from a fight. When I helped him clean off the stage makeup, I found an envelope in his trailer written in blood red letters. It said both of our names, our real names, and inside was the intimate photograph of us from the other night. The caption said there was more where that came from and that whenever the stalker was through with him, it wouldn't be fake blood pouring from his nose."

Hudson expelled a long breath. "Sonny, how do you know that this person isn't going to come after you?"

"I don't." She shrugged her shoulders. "I can only hope that now that I'm not affiliated with Daxton Knight I'm no longer a valuable way to target him."

"We can hope, but I'm not that reassured."

"As mad as I am at Dax and at Zola too, I would never wish anything negative to happen to them. I hope that Dax uses his head and goes to the authorities sooner than later."

Hudson nodded. "Of course, because you're a good person. Speaking of Zola, though. She is obviously jealous. Have you considered that maybe the threats are from her, to scare you two away from each other?"

"She just got into town this morning after flying over night from Paris. She wasn't in the area, and honestly, she strikes me as a person who would much rather complain than put any action behind it. But he obviously pissed off someone."

Hudson gestured to her. "More than one someone."

"You're right about that, but I know that I'm not sending him messages."

They both smiled.

"Are you going to be okay?"

"Yes, I will be. My ego just took a big hit. I'll recover."

"Anything that I can do to help? Buy you ice cream, alcohol?"

"You're too kind," she said as she reached into her purse to pull out her phone. "Ugh."

"What?"

"Lillian Grace has messaged me. She's been riding me about attending a dinner party tonight with some of the cast and crew. She won't take no for an answer."

"Maybe you shouldn't say no. Other people obviously want you there, and just because one door closed doesn't mean you should take it upon yourself to shut them all."

"Why would I go now? I'm not even an employee anymore."

"No, but you *are* a likeable person. You should make an appearance just to prove that you can."

"It'll be uncomfortable. I should just ignore her."

"First off, you do not ignore Lillian Grace, and secondly, let him be uncomfortable. You did nothing wrong and should hold your head high. At least call her back."

"You are just as persistent as she is."

"Go ahead, dial."

Sonny sighed and turned her back to him as she placed the call. "Lillian? Hi, it's Sonny."

Hudson could only hear Sonny's side of the conversation, but judging by what he could see, Lillian was doing most of the talking.

"Okay, I'll see you there."

Sonny hung up, and Hudson asked, "Well?"

Sonny grimaced. "I think I just got talked into going."

"Good."

"Wipe that smug look off of your face, you're also going. She told me I could bring a date."

CHAPTER 11

"Remind me again why we're going to this thing," Sonny said as she checked herself for the millionth time in the mirror.

"Stop fidgeting, you look beautiful," Hudson said. "You're going because you're an attractive single female who's an established hard-working individual who is looking to become a published author someday. You're a person who has a lot to offer. You're an equal to everyone who's in that room and, from what I've heard, you may even be better than some of them."

Sonny smiled at him appreciatively. But she still hesitated to get out of the car when he handed his keys to the valet.

"You know, in order to make a grand entrance, you kind of have to get out of the car."

"Right," she said and opened the door.

"Besides, it would be an awful waste seeing as how you changed your outfit nearly ten times."

She gave him a playful punch on the shoulder.

He faked being wounded. "Hey, I'm not saying it's a bad thing. I think you made the right choice." Hudson eyed her appreciatively. "Dax is going to eat his heart out when he sees you."

"You do wonders for my confidence. Thank you."

"That's what I'm here for."

He held out his arm, and she hooked hers through it. "Shall we?"

"We shall."

Sonny steadied herself on her heels and took a deep breath. She was completely unaware of how handsome they were as a duo. Hudson cleaned up nicely and was wearing a sharp suit and tie. She had to admit she was more than mildly impressed at how much he fit into the atmosphere and was incredibly grateful for his company. It didn't hurt matters that he wasn't ugly. It boosted her self-esteem that it appeared that she could get a hot date.

Hudson hadn't done badly for himself either as far as his escort to the event. Sonny wore her hair in tousled curls with one side pinned back. She had opted for a dress that had been hanging in her closet for over a year, but that she had never worn. It was sparkly and flashier than was her usual style, but she had gotten it on sale for no particular reason other than she liked it. The slinky material clung to her petite frame, accentuated the curve of her rear, and showed off her shapely legs.

Sonny had taken the time to make sure her makeup was perfectly in place, and no one would guess that instead of being airbrushed, it was purchased from the drug store. Her shoes were her only splurge, and the strappy buckled heels were worth every penny as it served to show off her toned calves. She ran her tongue over her teeth to make sure that the pink gloss was only where it needed to be.

"Ready?" Hudson asked.

"As I will ever be," she answered, and he opened the private banquet hall doors.

When they entered the room, it was abuzz with busy chatter, and Sonny thanked her good fortune that it was not nearly as formal and quiet as she had anticipated. Waiters dressed in all black walked around serving appetizers as the bartenders were busy mixing fancy cocktails.

She recognized a lot of the crew as they nodded their hellos. She plastered a smile on her face, but her eyes were busy scanning the room.

"Three o'clock by the window, and he looks positively thrilled to be entrapped in the conversation he is in," Hudson said.

Try as she might, Sonny's eyes involuntarily moved in that direction and, to her dismay, Dax was staring in astonishment back at her.

Sonny adverted her gaze, but she knew that he had seen her take notice.

"I think he's wondering what I'm doing here."

"No, I think his eyes are glued to that dress, along with every other man in this room with a pulse. They're shocked at what you normally hide, Ms. Winslow, and I must say so am I," Hudson praised her.

"Okay, we're in a room filled with actresses and models, so now I know you're talking out your ass. Let's get a drink."

"Yes, ma'am," he said and grabbed her hand.

"What are you doing?" she asked in a hushed tone.

"Making Mr. Knight jealous."

"He has nothing to be jealous of, and that's not why I came here, Romeo."

"I know that, but it's an added bonus, don't you think?"

"Whatever you say."

"Sonny," a voice said rather loudly. "I'm so glad you came."

Sonny turned to see Lillian approaching them. When she was directly in front of them, she gave air kisses to both of her cheeks.

"You look positively radiant," Lillian gushed.

"As do you, as always."

"You're too kind. Who is this handsome gentle-man?"

"Lillian Grace, this is Hudson Law, a fellow writer and artist as well as my roommate."

"It's a pleasure to meet you."

"Likewise," Hudson replied as he kissed her hand.

"A man with manners. I like that. So another writer, huh? I would love to read your work. I find the writing process fascinating."

"Thank you, it would be an honor."

"Oh, nonsense, the honor would be all mine. Sonny's going to let me get a sneak peek at her manuscript soon, aren't you?"

"Um, yes, of course," Sonny replied.

"You two need a drink. This is supposed to be a party, after all."

"We were on our way to do just that."

"Great. I'll join you, my drink could use refreshing."

As they walked toward the bar, Lillian asked, "How are you? You seemed pretty upset earlier."

"I'm fine. Thank you. My confidence level was a bit down, but I'm feeling much better."

"Good to hear. Have you talked to Dax?"

"No, I was actually hoping to avoid that, seeing as how it would be pretty awkward."

"Nonsense, Sonny. He would love to talk to you."

"I don't think that's such a good idea," Sonny said. "I don't think either of us has anything to say."

"Well, I know that to be untrue," Lillian said.

"What makes you so sure?"

"Because he was insistent that I get you here."

CHAPTER 12

Dax waited until Sonny was momentarily alone before he confronted her. She had slipped out into the hallway, and he followed behind her to where she let herself out of the side door. It gave way to an alley which, for the moment, was uninhabited. She rubbed her arms up and down to ward off the chill caused by the crisp night air.

"Are you cold?" he asked.

Sonny whipped her head around startled. "What are you doing here?"

"I didn't mean to scare you. I just wanted to talk for a second."

Sonny crossed her arms in front of her chest defensively. "Well, I have nothing to say to you."

"That's okay. I have a lot to say to you. So all you have to do is listen."

Dax was blocking the entrance back into the building, and she couldn't very well just walk away and leave Hudson inside, so she stood, trying to look indifferent to whatever he could possibly say.

Dax licked his lips before beginning. "I'm an ass. I know that. I speak without thinking. I only worry about myself. I'm selfish. And, although it has hindered some of my personal relationships over the years, ultimately it's what has worked for me. I have never felt guilty. Until now. I can't explain it, but knowing that I hurt you is eating me up inside. You didn't deserve to be treated like that, and I'm sorry. You may not believe me, but I didn't mean the things that I said. Quite the opposite actually. I don't know who I was trying to convince otherwise, Zola or myself. You're the farthest thing from a coat-tail rider. If your novel uses half of your wit, it will sell like hotcakes. You don't need me to do it, and I know that. You're not a charity case. That was a very hateful thing for me to say. You have helped me, more than the other way around. I find myself wanting your opinion, wanting to spend time with you. I care what you think." He shook his head. "That's new to me, and I didn't know how to handle it. You're so smart, beautiful, endearing—"

"Stop," Sonny said. Her eyes brimmed with tears. "Please stop."

Dax closed the space between them and gently but purposefully grabbed her arms. "No, you have to hear this. Please let me finish. You're a complete package, and anyone would be lucky to have you. Neither I, nor anyone else should ever make you feel less than you are. When I told Zola that there was no comparison between the two of you, I was right, but the other way around. Zola couldn't hold a candle to you, and she knows it. That's why she's so jealous. Through our phone conversations, she heard me speak very highly of you, and she hopped the first flight she could find to check you out for herself. You are anything but average. You're extraordinary. Zola has to rely solely on her looks, as do a lot of women who come on to me. I told you once that I liked a woman who had a brain in her head, and your mind impresses me almost as much as your body in that dress. You're gorgeous and don't need a team of professionals to make you that way, from that killer body that you've been holding out on, to the spray of freckles across the bridge of your nose. Beauty like that can't be faked. I don't expect you to forgive me right away, but I do want you to know that I'm sorry from the bottom of my heart. That's why I pestered Lillian to guilt you into coming here, so that I could tell you that. Now, will you please come back to work for me?"

Sonny had been stunned into silence at the words coming out of his mouth. "Wow, Dax that was some elaborate speech. Who wrote that for you? It was quite a performance."

He stared hard into her face. "I did rehearse what I wanted to say to you, many times, but the words are mine, and I meant every one of them. Please come back to work for me. It isn't the same without you."

"It has only been one day without me."

"And it's not the same. I need you on my team. I'll pay you double."

Sonny gaped at him. "You're crazy."

"And you're worth it."

"I can't be bought, Dax. I won't sacrifice my pride and self-worth for some extra money."

"I know, and you won't have to. We're equals, and you will be treated as such. You'll see."

Sonny bit the corner of her lip and exhaled in exasperation. "What do you think Zola will say?"

"I don't care what she has to say, quite frankly. I sent her back to the airport."

"You broke up with her?" Sonny asked incredulously.

"She wouldn't say that. She would claim it was all her idea, and that we just needed a break, some space to figure things out. Besides, 'No one breaks up with Zola and gets away with it,'' he said, mocking her accent.

Sonny couldn't help but smile. "I'm sure she's none too pleased. She probably thinks it's all my fault."

"I wouldn't worry too much about what Zola thinks. She just worries about herself. She'll move on to another poor soul in no time."

"You're a poor soul?" she asked with chagrin.

He attempted to give her his best wounded-puppy-dog face. "Maybe not, but maybe I want to be better than that. Do you forgive me? Will you give me another chance?"

Sonny lowered her gaze. "I absolutely do not forgive you, but we may be able to negotiate a pay raise that could work to both of our benefits."

"Great, I can work with that." He started to lean forward.

Sonny held up a hand to stop him. "Stop right there. I said I would think about it. I need to make sure it's the right move for me. And no more of this."

"What?" he asked with a boyish grin.

"No more innuendos, brash flirtations, invading my personal space. If you can't abide by my rules, then I'm most definitely out. I need time to think, and I don't need to become another mark in your little black book of conquests. Understand?"

Dax's smile faded, and he became serious. "Yes, I understand."

"Good." She shivered.

"Are you cold?"

"Slightly. I should probably go in. I left Hudson all alone. Although, I got the feeling that he would be just fine keeping himself entertained with all of the beautiful women inside."

"Why would he care about them when he has a date wearing a dress like that?"

Sonny looked at him in dismay.

"Sorry. I'm going to have to reprogram myself. It's not going to happen immediately."

He held the door open for her.

"One more thing, Dax."

"Yes?"

"I think that you need to be very careful and take your stalker seriously. I know that you may have come across some deranged fans in your time, but I have a feeling this person can be seriously dangerous."

"Yes, boss," Dax said with a mock salute.

Sonny spotted Hudson immediately. His gaze was inquisitive when he saw her company, and she rolled her eyes to answer his silent questions. She motioned for Dax to follow her for an introduction.

"There you are. I was looking for you," Hudson said.

Hudson had been involved in a conversation with Lillian and some of her friends.

Sonny smiled knowingly. "How hard did you look?"

He shrugged sheepishly.

"Hudson, this is Daxton Knight. Dax, this is Hudson Law."

The two men shook hands.

"So you're the new roommate," Dax said.

"So you are the well-known actor," Hudson said.

Dax smiled. "I guess you could say that."

The two men sized each other up in a friendly sort of way and must have come to a silent understanding because a moment passed and then the awkwardness dissipated.

Sonny was not privy to the male way of communicating, but it would seem these two had just had a conversation without words right in front of her.

Lillian interjected. “So, Sonny, I see that Dax found you. Will I be seeing you on set on Monday morning?”

Taken off guard, Sonny replied, “It’s a possibility. We’re still negotiating.”

Lillian smiled. “Well, give her whatever she wants, Dax. That’s my advice, and you would be smart to take it.”

“I’m doing my best,” Dax answered. “This one here is a tough one.”

“Maybe so,” Lillian mused. “But then again, so are you, and she’s earned the right to be tough.”

Somehow, Sonny had earned having Lillian in her corner, and she smiled in appreciation. “Are you about ready, Hudson? It’s getting late.”

Hudson looked around the room at all of the beautiful women taking advantage of the champagne and top-shelf liquor. “Yes, if you’re ready, then so am I,” he said with a mild undertone of regret.

Sonny knew he probably preferred to stay, but she wanted to leave before everyone’s inhibitions had completely gone by the wayside.

“I’ll get the car.” He started to excuse himself then stopped.

Sonny's phone buzzed in her clutch, and she started to silence it until she saw that Miles was calling. "I wonder what he could want at this time of night." She answered and turned away while plugging the opposite ear to hear over all of the commotion. "Hello?"

"Sonny." Miles sounded panicked.

"Yes, what is it?" she asked with dread.

"There's been an accident. We're all okay, but Vivian's being rushed to the hospital to check on the baby."

"Oh no, are you okay? The baby?"

Dax stepped up to grab her elbow, sensing her urgency. She held up a finger asking him to give her a moment.

"I'm okay, and Vivian is talking and seems to be okay as well, but she is complaining of back pain and cramping. It was a fender bender, someone hit us from behind. The driver hit us rather hard, and the doctors want to make sure the baby's not in distress. Oh, God, the baby's probably okay, right? Viv's dad and sister are coming, but I know she would want you to know."

Sonny could hear the panic in his voice. It was the sound of an inexperienced father trying to protect his family but not knowing what to do exactly.

"Of course, Miles. I'll be there as fast as I can. Calm down. Vivian and the baby need you. Think positive thoughts, Miles. Is she being transported to Mercy Medical?"

"Yeah," he said shakily, and Sonny thought he might be crying.

"I'm on my way." Sonny looked up at the small crowd watching her conversation. "I have to go. My friend Vivian was in a car accident and is eight months pregnant."

She started to walk away and realized she didn't have a car.

Hudson reacted immediately. "I'll get the car," he said again.

"I can take you," Dax said at the same time.

Sonny looked between them both. "You don't have to leave your party. I rode here with Hudson."

"Please, I want to. Inadvertently, I feel like I know the woman because she referred me to you."

"Either way, I'm going," Hudson said.

"Okay." Sonny grabbed Hudson's hand. "It's decided. Let's go, hurry."

She took off at a sprint to the valet.

ꕥ

Dax stood back and watched, feeling helpless and out of control, as the two disappeared.

"Wishing it was you?" Lillian asked.

"Not now, Lil. There's a baby's life at stake. I just wanted to help."

"If you want to show your support, go to her, even if it just means sitting in the waiting room. She'll appreciate the gesture more than you know."

"You're right," Dax said and chased after them.

When he got into his car, he shoved the gear into drive and started to take off. He noticed a photograph lying on his passenger seat. He reached for it immediately. It was a picture of a pregnant woman being loaded onto a stretcher. Dax's breath hitched in his throat. Presumably, he guessed, the patient's name was Vivian. His mouth went sour as he flipped the picture over. On the back written in felt tip marker read a caption:

Better watch what you touch before it all turns to shit.

"Shit, shit, shit," was all he could repeat the entire way to the hospital.

CHAPTER 13

When Sonny rushed into the hospital, she was directed to the fifth floor where she ran into a very nervous Miles in the hallway. He was pacing frantically making phone calls.

"Is she okay?" Sonny asked.

Miles's eyes were terrified and showed the all-consuming fear for the wellbeing of his wife and baby.

"They rushed Viv up here and are running some basic tests." He went on to explain further, before adding. "They assured me that the baby's heartbeat is strong, but they asked me to leave the room."

"I'm sure they have their reasons, Miles. That's very reassuring news. How's Vivian?"

"Nervous, but otherwise, I think she only has some minor cuts and bruises."

"And should I ask, how are you?" Sonny questioned him sympathetically.

"Me? I'm fine. Mad as hell that the bastard who hit us just took off after the accident."

"He just left?"

"Yes, peeled out. I was so concerned with my family, I didn't even get a look at the license plates or make and model of the car. If I ever get my hands on the person responsible—"

"Miles, that's terrible. But right now we just need to focus on Vivian and the baby."

Sonny knew he needed to direct his anger somewhere, and she didn't blame him one bit.

A nurse poked her head out of the room. "Sir, you can come back in now."

Sonny gave Miles's shoulders a gentle squeeze, and he took off to be at Vivian's side. "We'll be waiting if you need anything at all," she called after him. Sonny stood there for a moment, feeling useless, and wished there was something she could do. When she turned around to make her way back to the waiting room, she was surprised to see Dax standing there. "What are you doing here?"

"I wanted to make sure your friends were okay, be here for you if you needed it. I saw Hudson in the waiting room. He directed me here. I told him he could go if he wanted, that I would take you home. He stuck around. I don't think the guy trusts me. I guess you told him about me being a complete asshole?"

"Yeah, I guess you could say that. He was there. I needed a friend, and he listened to me."

"I'm glad he was there for you," Dax said quietly. "It makes sense that he would be skeptical of me and my intentions. How are your friends doing? Is the baby going to be okay?"

Sonny ran her hands through her hair. "The baby's heartbeat is strong and steady. Vivian appears to be stable. Miles said they were running some testing to be sure. Apparently, the accident caused Vivian to start having contractions. They're determining if it was actual labor or some Braxton hicks. They'd like to get a two-part steroid shot in her to help the baby's lungs develop further. Right now it's a waiting game and observation. Miles is a nervous wreck and directing his anger toward the driver of the vehicle that hit them."

"Do they know who hit them? Will they be able to file a police report when things settle down?"

"That's the terrible part. The driver was a hit and run. Miles was so busy being concerned with Viv and the baby that he didn't get a view of the license plate or even a visual on the vehicle."

"Sonny, I should really tell you something. Do you want to grab a cup of coffee while we wait?"

"What is it, Dax—"

The doors swung open abruptly to Vivian's room, and doctors surrounded her hospital bed as they rushed it down the hall with an air of urgency. The lights flashed to indicate an emergency situation as a code white was called to bring all hands on deck.

The white-coated personal yelled out stats down the corridor, and the surgeons and pediatric specialists ran past them to scrub in.

Miles was chasing behind them, looking lost and panic stricken. "They can't find the heartbeat, Sonny. Pray they find the baby's heartbeat," he yelled in distress.

"Dad, you have to wait out here until further notice. We will keep you abreast as we know more," a surgical nurse told him.

"That's my wife and my child. Are they going to be okay? Tell me they're going to be okay," he sobbed miserably.

Sonny ran to him.

"Ma'am, are you family?" the nurse asked her.

"Just let me comfort him. Please," Sonny said.

The nurse relented, and Sonny enveloped Miles in a compassionate embrace, trying to soothe his trembling body. "They're going to be okay. These doctors are trained for these events. It's going to be just fine. They were in the right place at the right time."

"She's losing a lot of blood. We are going to need to do a transfusion. Somebody get me some blood!" a doctor yelled.

"Baby is in acute distress. Heartrate is low. Mom's heartrate is also dropping. Come on, people, move. She's bleeding out."

"Oh, God, no!" Miles covered his face with his hands.

Suddenly, things got really quiet, and they strained with nervous anticipation on the other side of the door.

"Talk to me, someone tell me what is going on with the baby," the doctor said as he worked on Vivian.

"Suctioning now, sir. Stimulating sternum, we might have to bag him."

Suddenly a newborn wail echoed loudly, and Sonny thought she had never heard anything more beautiful. Tears rolled freely down Sonny's cheeks as she clasped her hands tightly around her face.

"He's breathing and with us," a voice called out. "Someone get me some oxygen."

"How's Mom?"

"She lost a lot of blood, but we're pumping her full again. I think she's going to be okay."

Sonny let out a long sigh and Miles cried openly. The anxiousness and relief exploded all at once.

"Oh, Miles." Sonny hugged him tightly. "It's all going to be okay."

The door swung open and a doctor adorned in scrubs, rubber gloves, and a mask peered into their tear streaked faces.

"You have a son. Would you like to come in and meet him?"

"Yes," Miles croaked.

"Follow me. Don't look to your right. Mom's going to be just fine, but we're stitching her up now and don't want you to see her that way. You can wait for her to wake up in recovery, but first, you need to meet your son."

"Oh, thank you, Lord." Miles clasped his hands together and turned toward Sonny.

She smiled in return. "Go, Miles, be with your baby. I can't wait to see you all together as a family."

And just like that, moments after the chaos erupted, the doors swung shut behind the world's newest father, and a strange quiet and calm settled over the buzzing unit.

Sonny stood for a while, feeling her own heartbeat return to normal, and listened to the sounds of her own breathing, lost in thought. She was so thankful for the positive outcome from such a high-stress, scary situation.

When she finally turned around Dax was waiting silently. He had been so quiet that she had almost completely forgotten he was there. She met his eyes, meeting emotion, and he wrapped her in a tight embrace. Allowing herself to be consumed by his comforting bear hug, she felt all of the fear escape through her sobs.

Dax held her silently, rubbing her back until the trembling subsided.

When she finally lifted her head, she said, "I'm sorry, I was so scared for them." Sonny pushed away, embarrassed.

"Don't do that," Dax said quietly.

"Do what?" Sonny said, wiping her noise with her sleeve.

"Apologize for being human. For caring so deeply about another family. It's admirable and nothing to be ashamed about."

Sonny stared deep into his eyes, and his sincerity melted her to the core. She leaned in, and all her reservations faded into the background. "Thank you for being here with me."

"I'm glad I didn't miss it," he said meaningfully.

His gaze had her transfixed into this one moment, and she could feel his breath on her face. She tilted her head, and his lips grazed hers as she invited him to kiss her and the doors swung open to the operating room.

A team of doctors pushed past them, rolling an incubator, and Miles followed behind them. He was now adorned in a surgical gown and mask of his own to protect his innocent newborn baby from any germs.

"We're headed to the NICU, the neonatal intensive care unit, so that he can be closely monitored, but he's doing great. He's four pounds already. Can you believe it?"

Miles beamed proudly. Stamped on his hand was the image of a tiny baby footprint and Sonny caught a quick glimpse of the new baby boy swaddled in blue. He had an oxygen cannula in his small little nostrils with tape that covered almost the entire sides of his petite cheeks, but he was beautiful.

"Oh, Miles, I'm so happy for you. He looks so strong."

"That he is, and so is his mom. Vivian will be in recovery soon. I can't wait to tell her how great she did and how perfect he is." His eyes shone with love for his bride and his new family. "I can't wait to tell Drew she has a baby brother. But I have to go so I can be back for when Viv wakes up."

"Of course, go."

"Thanks again for being here, Sonny. I don't know what I would have done if I was by myself. I probably would have freaked out. When she wakes up, she'll be sore and groggy, so tomorrow will probably be better for visitors."

"I'll definitely be back tomorrow. Congrats, Papa. Fatherhood looks good on you."

Miles turned to Dax. "Make sure she gets home, okay?"

"Of course. And congrats, man." Dax shook his hand enthusiastically. "It truly is beautiful."

ꕥ

They stood and watched as the new dad followed the incubator down the hall.

"Ready to go?" Dax asked.

Sonny sighed. "Yes, this has been an emotionally taxing day. I'm exhausted, and I'm not the one who gave birth or had emergency surgery."

Hudson left shortly after learning that all parties were going to be okay, and Sonny followed Dax out to his car. When she got into the passenger seat, she closed her eyes wearily. Dax had soft music playing that filled the car.

When they neared her house, she said, "I cannot wait to take off these shoes and this dress."

"Need some help with that?" he asked suggestively.

"You're ruthless," Sonny said.

"It was worth a try."

"About earlier," Sonny began. "I know I kind of leaned in, and, well, you know, but I was feeling vulnerable, and all of the emotion made me lose my head for a second. I still mean that we shouldn't cross the line—"

"Sonny, I understand." He stopped her. "Say no more. I'm just happy you're back on board," he said as he pulled in front of her house.

She smiled ruefully. "And I told you, I was still thinking about it."

"Didn't tonight earn me some points?"

"Yeah, yeah," she said. "You know something? You are awfully confusing."

"How so?"

"One minute I hate you and the next I—Well, the next I don't hate you. I can't figure you out."

He smiled. "Maybe, it's part of my mystique."

"Whatever you say."

She started to get out of the car, but the photograph lying underneath her caught her eye.

Dax held his breath.

"What the hell is this?" she yelled.

CHAPTER 14

Sonny, wait. Let me explain."

Dax scrambled to get out of the car before Sonny escaped into her building. He raced up the steps in time to almost collide with her when she whirled around. She didn't back down even when they were nose to nose.

Sonny poked her finger into his chest and pushed hard to force him to step back. "You. You're a liar. You came to the hospital because you got a message from your sick demented stalker telling you that they were behind the heinous act that caused my friends to have their baby ahead of schedule. That baby could have died. Vivian could have died. This psycho could have cost that family their lives. Do you get that?" she spat angrily.

"Look, Sonny. I know that you're upset. And rightfully so, but I did not lie to you. I wouldn't lie about something so serious. There wasn't a right moment to tell you, with everything going on. I planned to tell you. You have to believe that. I just—"

"Withheld important, no, imperative information. There would never be a good time to tell me. It's not the kind of news that would ever sound better, no matter how you try to spin it. My friends just went through a terrifying ordeal because of you. No, because of me getting involved with you. I told you to take this more seriously, that this deranged psycho is dangerous. Daxton Knight couldn't have this in the headlines. He didn't want to take attention away from his upcoming movies."

"Why are you talking about me in the third person?"

"You're intolerable."

"Listen, I'm not trying to make light of the situation. I found the photograph in my car as I was chasing you to the hospital to be by your side. After I found you, everything happened so fast, and there was no time." Dax grabbed her hands. "Sonny, I had no idea that this person was planning the accident or that they were capable of such violence. Until now they were all bark, but no bite. If I thought they would put action behind their threats, I would have reported it immediately."

"This all happened because I got involved with you and your madness." Sonny's voice cracked under the strain of the day's pressure. "I should have followed my instincts. I knew that this would never work out. Instead, I invited this chaos into my life with open arms. What was I thinking?"

Tears filled her voice, and she turned to go back inside. Dax grabbed her arm, and she hesitated.

"Sonny, please don't go. This isn't your fault. We couldn't have known. I didn't take it seriously enough, not until the messages started to involve you. I would never want to see you hurt or scared." Dax rubbed his thumb across the top of her hand. "Sonny, please, I know that maybe I haven't made the best impression, but I hope your instincts tell you that I'm not a bad guy. I may not have always been the nicest guy, but I never wanted any of this to affect you or those you love." His voice was gruff and full of feeling. It didn't just *matter* that she believed him. It was suddenly *necessary.* "Please trust me."

Sonny turned slowly with tears tracks streaked down her face. "Trust you?" she scoffed. "You must think that I'm a real idiot, don't you?"

"No, of course not."

"Save it, Dax. Call Zola and tell it to her. You two are one of a kind. You really do deserve each other."

"Zola?" Dax asked, confused. "What does she have to do with this?"

"You two enjoyed a good laugh at my expense. I'm only a waitress remember? This waitress was too blind to see the warning signs. Being around you is dangerous."

Sonny yanked her arm away and abruptly escaped to the confines of her apartment building with a quick and precise click of the door.

"Dammit," Dax yelled into the night.

It was too late, the day had proved to be longer than most, and seemingly everything that could have gone wrong, did. He should go home, drop into his bed, and sleep until this mess passed over him. A couple of weeks ago, he would have done just that.

Sonny didn't want to talk to him. She didn't trust him. He should cut his losses, find a new personal assistant, and move on. He could report his stalker to the police and let them do their job while he tried to do the best he could at his.

This was just a bump in the road. He could even smooth things over with Zola if he really wanted to. It probably wasn't too late to do some schmoozing. He wasn't interested in doing that, though.

There was no shortage of women who could help take his mind off of things, but he had been there and done that, and something told him that if he went that route, he would just feel worse. Yet here he was standing outside of Sonny's apartment, unable to go, and she was unwilling to hear him out.

He couldn't stand the fact that she was angry with him, but he was just as agitated that he couldn't let it go. This was uncharted territory for him. He stared at the God-forsaken photograph.

"Who are you, you prick? When I find you, I'll make you pay. That's a promise."

ഗ്ദ ഗ്ദ

Sonny let herself into her front door, and exhaustion overwhelmed her. She walked through the dark apartment, careful to avoid the corners of furniture, moving around them by memory. She flipped the light on to her bedroom once she had closed the door behind her. She supposed Hudson was already asleep as the house was enveloped in silence.

The normally welcomed reprieve was now eerie, and although being alone before had never bothered her, it was now too quiet to drown out the thoughts filling her head.

Why would someone go after an innocent family? What purpose did that serve? She was grateful that Baby Whitman was going to be okay, but the chaos and fear surrounding his birth made her angry.

She stripped from her dress, pulled a worn comfortable tee shirt from her dresser, and slid it over her head. When she lay back against her pillows, her body ached with mounting tension, and she felt depleted from used up adrenaline. She needed to sleep, and things would be more clear in the morning. She decided she would go to the police before swinging by the hospital to check on the new family. How quickly things had escalated from a simple overzealous fan producing hate mail.

She was angry at Dax but couldn't place the root of that anger. He had seemed concerned at the hospital, and she knew he couldn't have predicted this outcome, but his normal cavalier untouchable attitude couldn't smooth over the events of today.

Restless, but desperately needing sleep, Sonny rolled and shifted trying to get into a comfortable position. She moved to her belly and cradled her pillow between her hands. When her fingers felt the crinkly paper, she quickly pulled it out while sitting up. She flipped on the bedside lamp and dread filled her from head to toe. A new wave of adrenaline coursed through her veins as her heart thudded in her chest.

She read and reread the typed letters over and over.

Don't even think about going to the police if you want your loved ones to stay intact. I warned you once about Daxton Knight. He is a danger to all of those around him.

CHAPTER 15

Daxton Knight got everything he ever wanted and then some. The odds were stacked against him and, even after walking through shit, he came out smelling like a rose. It really wasn't fair, and he was no more deserving than anybody else. Some would argue he was even less so.

He had been able to let go of the past and move forward to bigger and better things—fame, fortune, a multitude of women. It was sickening, how he never looked back, never cared about those left in his wake.

He would care, and soon enough he would be reminded. There was a time when Daxton was just another smart-aleck poor boy who wasn't going anywhere, just like everyone else from their sleepy little town.

"I could never understand how teachers and classmates would take a special liking to him even when he spent so much time in the principal's office. Maybe if we had all been given the same time and special attention, we would have had a fighting chance to make something of ourselves, but no, Daxton was the shining star. It may have always been that way, but it stops now. The past always has a way of catching up with you."

ᘓᘐ

The morning sun was too bright on Dax's tired eyes, and the coffee wasn't strong enough or made specifically the way he liked it. There was no breakfast waiting for him, but it didn't matter anyway. He wasn't in the mood to eat.

Dax pulled his car into the busy hospital parking lot and, after circling the lot three times, finally found a spot. He waited impatiently for the car to back out and had to resist honking his horn at the old man after seeing him tap his brake lights with his over-cautious, slow-moving driving. Dax pulled into the spot and jumped out of his car with zeal as he half-walked, half-ran through the hospital's front doors.

At some point in the early morning hours, he had decided that Sonny's inability to forgive him was not good enough. This mad man was on the loose and, even if he had brought it into her life, it was too late now. This criminal knew where she lived, what she drove, and who she associated with. She wasn't safe, and it was his responsibility to make it right. He would insist that she see his point and let him help her.

He hit the button on the elevator for the third time and looked around in exasperation for the stairs. About the time that he was going to find a hospital personal, the elevator door opened and one lone person was staring back at him.

"What are you doing here?" Sonny asked, guarded.

"I needed to see you."

"I thought I made myself clear last night."

"I can't accept that."

"Can't or won't?" Sonny asked.

The doors began to close, and Dax pushed his hand between the heavy doors to open them back up. "Both, I can't, and I don't understand why, so I won't until I figure out why I can't just walk away."

"Get in," she said.

Dax stepped inside of the elevator. "Have you seen your friends? How are they today?"

"They were working on a feeding with the baby, so I was going to walk around and grab some coffee. He had a feeding tube that they fed him through throughout the night until Vivian felt up to trying on her own. The fact that he has a suckling reflex already is very promising, the doctors said. Their family was visiting so I didn't want to intrude."

"That's great news." Dax shoved his hands inside of his pockets. "Look, I know you're mad at me and think that this is all my fault, and I guess that, inadvertently, it is, but if I could have foreseen the future, I would have done everything in my power to stop it, but we are here now. I can't change it, and neither can you. We both would if we could, but this person is obviously capable of harm. They know where you live and have delivered a personal message to you once. They went after your friends. I can't just walk away from you, not knowing if you're going to be okay. I could never forgive myself if something happened to you because of me. As it stands, I'm going to have a hard enough time with that the way it is. So you can be pissed at me. But you can't push me away from you."

The elevator doors opened with a ding, and Sonny grabbed his shirt sleeve pulling him along with her. "Unfortunately, I agree. I think by befriending you, I'm already going to be punished."

"What do you mean?"

Sonny stopped short. "I received another message last night."

"What? After I left? I knew I shouldn't have left you alone. We have to take this to the cops."

"Ironically, that's exactly what the letter warned me not to do."

"What are you talking about?" he hissed.

She avoided his piercing gaze. "The warning couldn't have been more clear. It was left under my pillow and said more people would be hurt if I took it to the police."

"What are you leaving out?"

"Nothing, you know that our tormentor just hits below the belt. It just said that you were a danger to all those around you."

Dax slammed his fist into the wall beside him.

"Dax, don't. That's not going to solve anything. The wall will win every time. Don't hurt yourself."

"I feel so useless," he growled. "And last night you all but said this was my fault. So you must agree."

She bit her lip. "Things have a way of looking different in the morning. I was angry and confused. I still am, but I know that you would have done something if you had seen this coming. The baby's doing very well, even better than expected, so from here on out, we need to focus on what we can do."

"Which is what? I feel like our hands are tied."

"I'm still trying to figure that part out. With no license plates or visual description, we're kind of at a road block, but I feel like I'm in too deep to just walk away. This person was in my house and hurt my friends. It's personal to me now."

"I would think that you would want to stay as far away from me as possible."

"Trust me, I won't be jumping at the opportunity to be seen with you in public, but we're going to put our nose to the ground and squash this guy."

"I'm on board for that, but where do we even begin? We're no amateur detectives."

"Quite the contrary, Dax. We begin with whomever you have ever scorned."

Dax looked leery. "You must enjoy spending time with me."

"What makes you say that?"

"Because the list may be long."

She snorted. "Of that, we can be sure. We better get started."

CHAPTER 16

When the feeding was over, Sonny and Dax were invited to come into the hospital room. Miles looked relieved and beamed from ear to ear when he opened the door.

"Hey, how's everyone doing?" Sonny whispered.

"See for yourself. Don't be alarmed by the tube in his nose, it's just a feeding tube in case they have to supplement his feeds. He did amazing, as did Vivian, at the last feeding He latched on and fed like a champ. They warned us we would probably need to use special bottles, but natural instincts kicked in and his suck/breath reflexes worked like a charm. Please, come in, Vivian can't wait for you to meet him."

Sonny entered the room, already jewelry free and scrubbed up to the elbow. Vivian lay in the hospital bed, looking a bit tired but overall peaceful. She held the precious swaddled bundle close to her skin to help him maintain his body temperature, but when she saw Sonny, she lit up like a Christmas tree at the chance to show off her new son. "Sonny, I'm so glad you came."

"I wouldn't miss meeting my honorary nephew for the world. How are you feeling?"

"Sore, but, otherwise, I feel lucky and truly blessed." She held up the tiny baby whose pink innocent face showed he was sound asleep. "Do you want to hold him?"

"Of course, I do. Is it safe? I don't want to jeopardize anything."

"Yes, we can let visitors in at our discretion. Besides, you're family."

Sonny's eyes grew misty as she reached out for the infant. She stared down into his perfect miniature face. "He's absolutely beautiful, but is somebody going to tell me his name?"

Vivian laughed. "We named him after my maiden name, Sullivan Story Whitman. We will call him Sully."

"It's perfect. Little Sully, you are one lucky boy to have such loving parents."

"Remind him of that when he's a teenager."

The women shared a smile, and Vivian looked past her at Dax. "Mr. Knight, it's a pleasure to finally meet you. I would get up, but the nurses practically have me chained to the bed."

"Understandable from what you have been through. Congratulations on your strong son. It's my understanding that he's a fighter just like his mama. I hope you don't mind my being here. I followed Sonny here last night and wanted to make sure you were all okay."

"It's perfectly fine. Any friend of Sonny's is a friend of ours. Besides, I'm honored to meet you after hearing so much about you from your agent, Maggie. It's not every day a movie star visits you in the hospital."

"Well, the honor is all mine, and don't believe everything Maggie says. I appreciate you recommending Sonny. She's been a real treasure."

"On that, we can most certainly agree." Vivian smiled, and Sonny blushed uncomfortably.

"Our focus should be on this beautiful baby," Sonny said. "So, Sully, why the middle name Story?" she cooed to him.

"We named him that because of all the sleepless nights I sat up reading my favorite story toward the end of my pregnancy." She looked meaningfully at Sonny. "You can't say you don't see some similarities from your manuscript. Sonny, we named him that after your story."

Sonny looked away, taken aback by the incredible honor, letting the tears flow freely down her cheeks.

CHAPTER 17

I'm surprised you didn't tell them about the person who ran them off of the road."

"It wasn't the right time. They're so happy and concentrated on their new family, as they should be. I didn't want to take anything away from the joy they have every right to be experiencing."

Dax nodded his head in understanding.

"You don't think that Zola has any connection to these vile messages do you?" Sonny asked as she looked out the window of Dax's car.

"Zola? I would find it highly unlikely. She may be a lot of things, but I don't think she is capable of thinking past what she's doing five minutes from now, much less have the sophistication to pull off all of these messages and planned attacks."

"But she was supposed to be at the party last night

before you basically uninvited her. A woman scorned is capable of a lot of things."

"Yes, but we were just beginning to spend time together when the first messages appeared. We were, in her words, in the honeymoon phase. She would have had no reason to be hateful then. In her mind, we were going to be the 'it' Hollywood couple, so why would she go out of her way to sabotage something that she seemingly wanted?"

"To make headlines? I agree the timing doesn't quite make sense, but we have to start somewhere."

They drove in silence for quite some time.

"Naming their baby's middle name after you was very sweet. You book must have really resonated with them."

Sonny looked at him quietly. "I guess some similarities spoke to Vivian. It's an honor that I will not take lightly. That baby is not even a day old and has my heart."

"You looked like a natural holding him so peacefully. Do you want kids?"

The question surprised her. "Someday, I suppose, if I meet the right person to have them with. What about you? You think you can settle down long enough to meet a nice girl and have a family?"

"It's a nice dream to have. In case you haven't noticed, I can be a little rough around the edges. I'm not sure if I'm cut out for that life, as appealing as it might be. I'm sure I would find a way to screw it up."

Sonny pondered the revelation and decided not to probe. That would generate a deeper conversation, one that could lead to dangerous waters, so it was best to steer clear and focus on the real-and-now issue that haunted them both. "Let's stop in at the café and grab a coffee. I need to reenergize."

After assuring all of Vivian's employees that things were going to be okay, Sonny and Dax chose a corner booth where their words wouldn't be overheard.

"So you had an assistant before me, Rachel, I believe you said."

"Yes."

"Romantically, intimately."

"Yes."

"Okay, and how did that end?"

"Look, if you want to hear me say that I loved her, and it just didn't work out, that's not going to happen. She was available, and we had sex. It was two consenting adults. She grew feelings, and I did not. About that time, I was being pursued by Zola, and in typical insensitive man fashion, I chose the super model. We tried to go back to working professionally as we had before, but it was too much for her, so she resigned."

"Resigned or was fired?"

"Neither really. A conversation was had, and the decision for her to move on was reached."

"Mutually agreed upon?"

"Look, Zola pushed for it, and to save the girl's feelings, I gave her a hefty severance pay, and she went on her way. I explained that I hoped there were no hard feelings, but I'm sure her ego was bruised, and I don't blame her. At the end of the day, it was just fun and games, and the feelings weren't mutual."

"All fun and games until someone gets hurt," Sonny mused.

"Rachel was a sweet innocent girl. I blame myself for taking advantage when I saw the stars in her eyes, but she's a good person, incapable of the deceitful, ugly messages and torment. I would rather leave her out of our twisted investigation."

"Okay." Sonny held up her hands in surrender. "I'm sorry to pry, but you seem to have a pattern forming here, and I was trying to look at this objectively from all angles."

"A pattern of hurting innocent people. Am I really such a monster that everyone who comes in contact with me is in danger?"

"I didn't say that," Sonny said quietly.

Dax's mouth was set in a hard line. "You didn't have to."

"I'm not trying to make you the bad guy. The stalker is the one victimizing innocent people, but there has to be a reason why. Have you ever beat out anyone for a role who would harvest a grudge?"

"I'm sure. We all get disappointed when we get passed over for a role, but we don't' go on a manhunt."

"Sane, logical people don't, but that's not who we're dealing with."

They stared into their cooling cups of brew when Hudson appeared at their table. "Hi, Sonny. Dax." He nodded. "How's Vivian and the baby doing? I didn't see you this morning before you left."

"I know. I was in a rush to get to the hospital. They really are doing much better. Doctors said they're hoping they're out of the woods and Sullivan will continue to thrive."

"That's fantastic news. I was really worried."

"We all were. Thank God our prayers are being answered and, hopefully, they'll all be out of the hospital soon."

"That's really great. I was just getting a refill. You just missed Nate."

"Oh, well, tell him I said hello."

"Who's Nate?" Dax asked.

"A fellow writer trying to make a name for himself. I think he has a little crush on Sonny. He'll be sorry he missed you."

Sonny's cheek instantly reddened.

"Oh, is that right?"

"He finds reasons to get together with me, but I think he is secretively hoping Sonny will be around." Hudson winked in conspiracy.

"Oh, Hudson, you're just reading into things."

"Whatever you say. I'll catch you guys later. Good to hear about Viv and the baby."

Sonny hung her head and looked at her hands.

When Hudson was out of earshot, Dax said, "You haven't mentioned this guy before. Why is that?"

"What do you mean? I don't have to tell you everything, you know. Besides, I barely know the guy. He's just friends with my roommate, which by the way he's entitled to be friends with whoever he wants. He doesn't need our permission."

"Well, that roommate seems to think this guy has a thing for you, which is my business."

"How do you figure?" she asked testily. "I don't see how this has anything to do with you."

"Because, at this point, anyone who comes into our lives unexpectedly may not be that innocent, nor that unexpected."

"Oh, I see. I guess it never occurred to you that someone could just meet me and find me interesting without having an ulterior motive. Of course, they would be up to no good and be more interested in you and your life. Is it really too much to think that a guy could really want me? I mean you really are so egotistical. This world is not always all about you."

"Whoa, slow down. It comes as no surprise that a man would be interested in you. Quite frankly, I would be more surprised if he wasn't. If his manhood is in working condition, then, of course, he wants you. What guy wouldn't?"

"So a man couldn't be interested in my mind or humor. It has to be physical, all about sex. What is it with you? Are you still going through puberty?"

"Quit putting words in my mouth. That's not what I'm saying. You're smart and funny along with a lot of other qualities that are both attractive and frustrating, but don't over estimate any man's ability to make anything sexual. It's the first way we decide if a chick is worth our time. Do we want to sleep with her or not? If the answer is yes, then we have to decide if there is more to her than a good time in the bedroom, but make no mistake, lust always comes first."

"You're disgusting, you know that?"

"Look, I'm not trying to be crude, just honest. Besides, why are you so defensive? Do you like this guy, Nate?"

"Dax, it's none of your business, but I don't know him. How can I like someone that I know absolutely nothing about?"

"You're right. It *is* none of my business, but someone is after us. I just want you to be careful. I would give you the same spiel about Hudson, but he was obviously your date at the time of the car accident last night so unless he has someone working with him, than that pretty much rules him out."

"Hudson was already ruled out. He's a good person."

"But what do you really know about him?"

"Look why are you questioning him? You just said he was ruled out. So why go there with an innocent person? He doesn't deserve to put under our microscope to be scrutinized."

"There you go getting defensive again."

"I just don't know why we're wasting our time."

"So my past relationships or sexual history can be discussed openly, but yours are off limits?"

She stared at him, incredulous. "I'm not in a relationship, and I'm not having sex with any of these men." She raised her voice, causing a few curious onlookers to take notice.

"So who are you having sex with?"

She lowered her voice to a dangerous whisper. "Once again, that's none of your business."

"I'm just wondering what is this act you have going? You return my kisses passionately and then go all cold on me like you're the Virgin Mary. Then go get all angry when I question two other men in your life. Maybe you should ask yourself about the company you keep and are you misleading or do you enjoy being a tease?"

Sonny stood suddenly. "Where do you get off? You have no right to question any of my behavior, especially when it's not warranted, but screw you for the insinuation that I'm a slut."

She stormed out of the café and stomped down the

side walk. Dax cursed and got up quickly to chase after her.

"Sonny, stop. Wait."

She picked up the pace.

"Would you slow down?" Dax grabbed her arm and spun her around. "Stop, Sonny. I'm an ass. I didn't mean it. I just want you to be extra aware of your surroundings." He grabbed her face in his hands. "I don't want anything to happen to you."

"That's what this is about?" she asked, tears shining unshed. "You're worried about my safety, so you act like I'm a scandalous whore?"

"No, I'm concerned about your safety, and I'm a jealous ass."

He kissed her tenderly on the forehead.

"Don't," she whispered.

He looked deep into her eyes. "Okay, I won't."

He reached out a hand to lead her to his car, and she gingerly accepted. *So much for not making a public skeptical of ourselves*, she thought.

ꕥꕥ

Beverly looked at the number Parker had given her, multiple times. She flipped the piece of paper over and over in her hands as if searching for a secret message that would suddenly appear. She even paced her apartment, carrying the cordless phone, turning it on, and punching in the first few digits, only to hang up before the call went through.

What was she doing? She was about to be a married woman. She had accepted a marriage proposal from another man with a ring to prove it. Beverly had said yes to spending the rest of her life with Steven, someone she knew she had loved. So why was she thinking about a complete stranger?

It had to be a case of pre wedding jitters, right? The simple solution was that her nerves were getting to her. She couldn't allow herself to get caught up in the hype of second guessing herself or the assumption that the grass was always greener on the other side.

Parker was just a brazen, cocky author who thrived on a challenge. It was some twisted game of manipulation, and she wouldn't allow herself to fall victim to it. Her happiness depended on her forgetting the tall, dark, and unruly stranger.

Steven was successful and by the book—everything she thought she always wanted. He was a scheduled, nine-to-five office man. She wouldn't have to worry about late hours or a moody artist that had to work through writer's block.

Parker was dangerous, and his eyes suggested he was unpredictable and lacked the proper manners. He wouldn't follow the rules and say all the right things in public settings.

If she married—no, *when* she married—Steven, she

would be envied and admired by all her nearest and dearest. Life would be stable and secure. That counted, right? Stability and practicality mattered. So why did it suddenly seem so mundane and boring? She needed to shake this self-doubt and plant her feet firmly in her designer wedding shoes that she would soon be wearing as she sauntered down the aisle to be Mrs. Steven Calvird.

In the past when she was feeling overwhelmed, she used an old technique given to her by her track coach. Visualize everything you are supposed to do. Walk through every motion in your mind and picture yourself doing it perfectly. Then when you go to perform it, it will be like second nature because, in your mind, you have done it a thousand times before.

The technique usually worked, but she had one small problem. When she visualized her wedding day, she pictured wearing the white dress that would be perfectly altered to her measurements. Her hair would be styled exactly the way they had practiced, and her sling backs would glide easily on her pedicured feet. She would hold the array of beautiful flowers that were fresh and delivered the morning of. She would watch her bridesmaids walk down the aisle to music she had picked out. Then all of her loved ones would stand as the music changed, and she was about to make her grand entrance.

She would keep her eyes on the groom and smile, maybe dabbing at a lone tear that escaped through her water-proof mascara. It would make for a memorable picture that would one day hang above their mantle. That picture would be frozen in time, and people would comment on the lovely memory when she welcomed them into her home. One day beside it would be pictures of their children, one boy and one girl, and they would look at it with happy hearts as they sat around the Christmas tree and recounted their many blessings.

Then the problem occurred. She looked up to meet Steven's eyes at the front of the chapel, only to find he wasn't there. It wasn't Steven at all.

She had to walk, had to get away from her apartment, away from the phone, and away from the lousy piece of paper that was clouding her judgement and had the power to potentially screw up everything she thought she had ever wanted.

Coffee, she would go out and get coffee.

Beverly walked the familiar streets and smiled at the familiar barista that knew her order and always made it just the way she liked it without having to ask her.

She was waiting for the comforting drink when a voice startled her from over her shoulder.

"Beverly. Fancy meeting you here."

She turned, knowing just who the baritone voice belonged to.

"I was afraid I would never see you again," Parker said.

"Why do I think that this was not a chance encounter?"

He shrugged nonchalantly, hands in his pockets. "Sometimes, you can't leave things up to chance."

She looked into his knowing eyes, the left one slightly bruised from the right hook that had been delivered by her future husband.

"What brings you out on this nice day?" he asked in his easy going manner.

"I needed a walk," she replied meekly.

Parker responded, "I like to walk."

She nodded a silent agreement before she could stop herself.

ꕥꕥ

"Cut. I think we got it," the director yelled.

"Great work today," Lillian said.

"Thanks, you too," Dax replied.

"I see that Sonny's back on the scene. You must have done some major convincing to get her to come back."

"I did my best. Although, I keep finding myself in the dog house."

"Old habits die hard, I suppose. But it's never too late to make some changes."

Dax looked around. "I hope so."

"Some things are worth changing for."

"When did you become so wise?"

Lillian smiled, rueful.

"You both did great. I can really see the plot coming together," Sonny said, walking over to them.

"Thanks, darling. You know what else is great? That manuscript that you sent me."

"Wait, what? You read my manuscript?"

"Yes, you emailed it to me, silly. It was the best thing I've gotten my hands on in a long time. The story really spoke to my heart."

Sonny blushed furiously as she tried to figure out how her manuscript had been sent when she did not do it herself.

"I mean it, Sonny. You're very talented. I have read many scripts in my life, and I know a good one when I see one. Don't sell yourself short. It was thought provoking, and I shed real tears. What a beautiful story."

"Thank you. I appreciate your feedback."

"I would recommend it to everyone. Let me know if I can help in anyway. It was an honor to read it."

Dax smiled. "Seems like Lillian Grace can't quit gushing over the up and coming author. Maybe it's time I took a look at it."

"Yeah, maybe." Sonny hesitated. "Are you ready to go? I actually have some writing to get to tonight if you don't mind."

"Okay, let me get out of my costume, and I'll be ready to go."

When Sonny got to the car, an envelope was tucked underneath the windshield wiper. Her heart immediately began to race. With trembling hands, she pulled out a photograph.

"Whatcha got there?" Dax asked. When Sonny turned, he saw the look of panic written all over her face. He dropped his bag and went to her immediately. "Sonny, what is it? Are you okay?"

She held up the photograph taken of the innocent kiss Dax had laid upon her forehead outside of the café. Scrawled across the picture was a message that read:

Do you really want this to get out?

"Is it ever going to stop?" she cried out. "What have we done to deserve this?"

"Sonny, I'm so sorry to have brought you into this mess. What can I do?"

"We obviously can't do anything. There are eyes and cameras everywhere. I wanted my name to be familiar to the world, but because people enjoyed reading my books, not like this. I never wanted this kind of attention."

"I know, and I'm sorry. Sweetheart, we're going to figure this thing out. I promise you. You—we—have nothing to be ashamed about. I don't care if it does get leaked. It was an innocent moment. I don't care who knows I'm spending time with you."

"Yes, you do. You've said as much. You and I are going to be humiliated and scrutinized and put on display."

"Sonny, listen to me. I could never be embarrassed

about you. You're the most normal person in my life. Please don't be intimidated into walking away."

"Can we please just go? I want to lock myself away from prying eyes, at least for a little while."

"Yes, we can go." Dax took the keys and opened the door for her. "We're going to my apartment and locking ourselves away."

Sonny started to protest, but Dax said, "Do you have a better solution?" Coming up with none, he took her silence as an agreement. When they were safely in the confines of the car and driving down the highway, Dax finally spoke. "On a lighter note, Lillian really seemed to like your book. I didn't know that you sent it to her."

"I didn't," Sonny said. "But I've got a good idea who did. Lillian and Hudson did an awful lot of talking at the party, and he's the only one with access to my computer."

"Does that make you angry?" Dax inquired. "I'm sure he was just trying to help."

"Angry, no. Perplexed, a little. I'm sure he had the best of intentions, and I'm less aggravated since the reception was good. If her rave reviews were more critiques, I might be slightly more annoyed, but that doesn't change the fact that I'm going to call him out on it. It's my baby to choose to share or not."

"I get that. Do you think you might choose to share it with me sometime?"

"Doubtful. I'm not really the coat-tail-riding type."

He grimaced as the harshness of his words once again came back to haunt him. "Sonny, I have not always said the right things to you, but I really do think highly of you, I want you to know."

"Yeah, I'm sure you do, but only after assuming I was trying to use your fame for my own notoriety and that I was a slacker waitress on the road to nowhere. I could see how associating yourself with me instead of a super model could be embarrassing, especially after thinking I was a slut. You would at least get some kind of compensation, but now the disappointment of learning that I'm just a kill joy and a tease who is naïve and stupid enough to hang around after being warned on multiple occasions by a secret stalker that you're dangerous and I should stay away. Instead, what do I do, but go and get photographed in a compromising position, in a public setting, nonetheless? I'm really proving myself to be a bright intellect. I can see why you have such a high opinion of me," she said sarcastically. "I can barely recognize myself."

"Stop it. Stop, Sonny. Don't do this to yourself. Don't let someone else's wrong doings dictate how you feel about yourself. Especially mine." He sighed. "I have no room to talk about anybody. I was a nobody, a trouble maker on the wrong track, and going down fast. I got lucky that some teachers saw some potential way down deep and forced me to graduate. They encouraged me to go on auditions after seeing me in the school play. Mind you, I was only supposed to be a stage hand as punishment, and they figured it was more likely to help me than afternoons filled with detentions. I was even luckier still when I caught my big break, and if I'm not careful, I still don't believe it. There are times that I wonder how I got here and if they haven't made a mistake by believing in me. They certainly believed in me more than I could have ever done for myself. Make no mistake, I was a shithead who was mad at the world, and, in some part of me, that boy still exists. It's not you who should be questioning yourself, but me. I'm trying to be a different, better person, but I've used people, hurt people, done things I'm not proud of. I have never pretended to be a saint. There are things that I've done that have made me ashamed. I'm ashamed of the way I've treated you. The last thing I want to do is hurt you."

Sonny sat quietly in his car, listening to his narration, debating over her inner struggle to trust him or not. "Why were you angry?"

"What?" he asked.

They were in the parking garage to his apartment now, but neither of them made a move to get out of the car.

"What were you so angry about as a kid, Dax? What inner turmoil do you harbor?"

"You are too perceptive for your own good, Sonny." He brushed a piece of hair away from her face.

"Don't change the subject by trying to charm me, Dax. I want to know."

He sighed in frustration. "My mom wasn't what you would call the holy grail of moms. She wasn't a member of the PTA. Hell, she didn't even go to my parent-teacher conferences. She slept her way through town, and everybody knew it. When I was old enough, it was even the talk of the locker room. I was teased relentlessly from other guys about how my mom woke up with *their* father instead of *mine* for breakfast. The other women hated her. I believe she destroyed some marriages along the way. I never knew my father, and she probably didn't either. She was a floozy, and I was her bastard son, and that didn't really earn us any points on the popularity contest. I was embarrassed by her and couldn't understand why just living life with me wasn't enough. When she had too much to drink, which was often, she would say awful things about how I was an accident, and if she could go back and terminate the pregnancy, she would. She would sober up and apologize. Make no mistake, men liked her because she was easy, but she also had a sweet childlike side to her. She was lost, and we all knew it. She finally settled down with a guy named Ray. He and his wife were separated, and he promptly filed for divorce after meeting my mom. He had a son the same age as me. His name was Mikey, but we never really hit it off. He spent most of his time with his mom, which was just as well.

"My mom and Ray drank too much, and one day on their way home from the bar, it all caught up. They spun out on some gravel, and a tree caught them. They were airlifted to the hospital, but my mom never made it out of the intensive care. She woke long enough on her death bed to give me a vague apology about leaving me alone in the world. For the first time, she admitted to me that she had been sexually abused by her stepbrother growing up. It explained a lot of things over the years and that she was just incapable of the kind of love a mother could give. I held her hand as she passed and was one of the few mourners at her funeral. I almost thought I could hear half the town breathe a sigh of relief when she died. But I knew she was a troubled soul. When Ray was released from the hospital and escaped charges for vehicular manslaughter, as no one was fighting on her behalf to see him put behind bars, he took me in as some kind of guilt. I think he thought if he provided shelter and food, that would be enough to abolish him of his sins.

"I didn't hate Ray, but don't get me wrong, there was no love lost when I moved out right after graduation. He did what he had to do, but nothing beyond that. I served as a constant reminder of his wrong doing, and he was relieved to move on with his life. To answer your question, I was angry at my mom. I was angry that she earned us both a reputation that I didn't deserve and had to overcome. I was angry that she had to endure what her stepbrother did and had suffered in silence. And I was angry that, when a true apology actually escaped her lips, she died shortly thereafter, leaving me in the lonely hellhole to fend for myself. And my outlet for that anger was everybody and everything.

"As I've gotten older, I've been able to refine the rough edges and realize how lucky I am to have been given opportunities, but it hasn't changed the fact that it has hindered my personal relationships. I sleep with too many women and never get too attached. I have broken hearts and lead people on. Just because I have stars behind my name doesn't mean that I'm not doing the very things that I hated. Maybe I come by it honestly, but I would like to think I could do better."

When he finally quit talking, the silence that engulfed them was deafening. They had been sitting in his car for a long time.

"Say something," he said. "Do you want me to take you home now?"

"No," she whispered. She covered his hand with hers. "I want to go upstairs with you and have dinner."

"Really?"

"Yes, I do. And you can do better. You can be anything or anybody that you want. You didn't fool anyone, you were given chances because of what people saw in you—the good that they saw and that I have seen, even around the rough edges."

His eyes shone bright with feeling. “Thank you,” he said gruffly as he rubbed the pad of his thumb across her cheek.

“Come on.” She grabbed his hand. “Let’s get something to eat.”

CHAPTER 18

After dinner, Sonny got up to clear the dishes away. She started to run water over the plates when Dax came up behind her. She could feel his commanding presence, even though he didn't touch her. The electricity was undeniable, and she didn't move, for fear that the slightest point of contact would create a spark, and that spark would catch fire. Once the fire was ablaze, she was uncertain if it could be fanned out.

Something about the way he had opened up to her made him all the more human, and she was hesitant to let herself see him that way. He could be hard to read and, at moments, even harsh, but when he revealed his past to her, the raw emotion that she saw was enough for her heart to break for him. She wanted to weep for young Daxton, and she wasn't sure what she wanted from Daxton Knight, the man, but the yearning in her abdomen told her she couldn't be too cautious.

She held her breath as they stood like that for long moments, each waiting to see what the other might do.

"Daxton," she finally said.

"Yes, Sonny."

"Don't."

"Don't what?" he whispered. His breath was on her neck.

"Don't make me explain things to you. Please just don't go there."

She closed her eyes as he reached into the warm water to take her hands. He interlaced his fingers through hers and gently rubbed his nose across the back of her neck, causing goosebumps to go up and down her spine.

"Dax, please," she said quietly, not even knowing herself what she was asking.

Slowly, he grabbed the washcloth and backed away. "Okay, I won't. Go take a bath or something. I promise not to bombard you. Relax, and I'll take care of this."

She turned to face him slowly, and he made no move to get out of her way. He had no intentions of making this any easier on her.

She met his eyes and recognized the shadow that crossed over his face. She needed to move, to get away. "Dax, I can't do this."

She slid past him, their bodies brushing against each other as she did. He sucked in his breath, and she hurried from the room.

As she filled the bath water, she clicked the lock on the door as a safety measure for the both of them. Sonny took a look at herself in the mirror and rolled her eyes at her reflection. Needing to focus her attention on something else, she picked up her cell phone and dialed Hudson.

"Hello? Where are you?" he answered.

"I'm at Dax's. It was a late night and going to be an early morning, so I'm just going to crash here."

"I'm glad you called. I was a little worried," he said, relieved.

"I know, and I didn't want you to be. I'm fine, but I do have a bone to pick with you."

"Uh, oh. Did you talk to Lillian?"

"So it *was* you who sent her my manuscript?"

"Please don't be mad. She seemed genuinely interested, and I thought it could help. When your computer was left open, I took a chance. I knew you probably wouldn't. I'm sorry if I overstepped my bounds."

"I know you were just trying to help, but it would have been nice if you cleared it with me first."

"I know. I'm sorry. What did she think?"

"She loved it."

"That's great. Maybe she can get it in the right hands."

"I guess we'll see."

"So when you're published, you can thank me then."

"If and when that happens, I'll remember that."

"But from now on you want me to go through you?"

"Yes, please," she said.

"Understood. Hey, there's someone here who wants to say hello."

"Who is that?" she asked.

"Nate is over here watching the game."

"Oh, yeah? Tell him I said the Cards are going to clinch it."

"I'll be sure to relay the message."

"Okay, I'll see you tomorrow."

"Sure. And Sonny?"

"Yes?"

"Be careful."

She hesitated. "I always am," she lied and hung up the phone.

She slid beneath the bubbles, his warning lingering in her ears.

ଓଡଓଡ

Sonny tossed and turned all night on sheets that smelled of Dax. He had let her have the bed, and he took the couch, but being under the same roof, although in different rooms, had not helped much.

When she woke in the morning, he was standing beside the bed holding a cup of coffee. "How did you sleep?"

"Great, thanks," she fibbed.

"Yeah, me too," he also lied.

He stood by the bed a moment too long, and she subconsciously swung her legs over the side and accepted the caffeine awaiting her.

"Well, it's an early call. We better get going."

When they walked out the door, cameras flashed in their face surprising them.

"Are you two a couple?"

"How long has this secret relationship been going on?"

"Is it true that you broke up with Zola Wallace because you're having an affair with your assistant?"

The cameras bombarded them, and Dax shielded her from the aggressive reporters. "What the hell are you guys doing here?" he demanded as he rushed them to their car.

"Are you aware of your intimate moment being released to the press?"

One reporter held a magazine, and their photograph was the headlining story. Dax snatched it from him before slamming the car door and squealing out of the parking lot.

"I cannot believe this," Sonny yelled. "It says an anonymous source confirms that Daxton Knight has a thing for his hired help. First, Rachel, and now a new woman, Sonny Winslow. Source says it must be serious as he reportedly broke up with super model Zola Wallace in order to pursue Ms. Winslow."

"Sonny, it's going to be all right. It'll blow over. It always does. I just can't believe that the bastard actually followed through with it."

Sonny was shaking by the time they arrived on set, and as Dax put the car in park, she covered her face in her hands.

"Sonny, don't. Who cares what people think?" He lifted her face in his hands. "Besides is being linked to me that terrible?"

She didn't answer him as they walked into the studio.

When Lillian saw them, she said, "Well, it looks like you two have had quite the eventful morning."

Parker was hesitant to leave Beverly, not knowing if he would ever see her again. He had done some investigating of her most common hang-out spots so that he could arrange the run in at the coffee shop.

The day they spent together was one that he would never forget, but as the sun went down her anxiety was apparent.

"Parker, I've enjoyed spending time with you, but this really isn't right. I'm engaged to another man."

"Have you ever thought it was the wrong man?"

"Don't do that."

"Do what?"

"Make me second guess everything I know to be right over two silly encounters."

"That's just it, Bev. You know it isn't right. Otherwise, why did you bother spending the day with me? You're questioning it too. You know you're making the wrong decision."

"I do not and quit saying that. I love Steven, and he loves me." She raised her voice.

"Not the way you should be loved. Not with the passion that I feel. You can't deny that."

"Life isn't just about passion and doing what you want to do all of the time."

"Are you listening to yourself? You know how crazy that sounds? What is it that you want to do but won't let yourself?"

"I don't know," she said miserably. "I think that you do."

Parker grabbed her face fiercely and claimed her lips with his. She let go of all reservations and returned his kiss passionately.

When they broke apart, her eyes were full of tears.

"Now tell me you didn't feel anything."

She couldn't bring herself to say the words, but tears streamed down her face. "I have to go. My fiancé is waiting for me."

Beverly turned and walked away.

"Dammit," Parker swore after her. "You're lying to yourself, and you know it."

ℭℭ

When the scene ended, Lillian wiped her face with a Kleenex, and Sonny did the same from behind the camera.

"How was that for acting?" Lillian asked.

"It was raw and intense. You both portrayed such emotion that it was almost hard to watch," Sonny said honestly.

"What about you, Dax? How do you feel about the scene?" Lillian asked.

Dax looked directly at Sonny. "I think that, in this case, 'Sometimes life does imitate art.'"

Sonny looked away, catching his meaning, and knowing it was all too true.

CHAPTER 19

How are you holding up?

Sonny turned from her spot where she waited for Dax to return from his trailer. "Lillian, hey. I'm doing all right."

"You don't have to lie to me. Given the circumstances, you have every right to be overwhelmed. It still gets to me on occasion, and I've had enough practice with it to last a lifetime."

Sonny sighed. "Well, it doesn't help matters that the reports are completely false. I've never been the girl who people look at when she walks into the room. And I've always been okay with that. I've always been more of the brains rather than the beauty, but lately, I haven't been living up to using my head either. I don't know what's wrong with me. I'm just hoping this attention will pass quickly."

"Oh, honey. It will. You just have to wait for the next big story to hit, and the attention will shift. Some people live to be in the headlines, but Dax is different. He does his best to always fly below the radar. But there are a couple of things that you said that are not completely true."

"Oh yeah, what's that?"

"First off, you are beautiful. You have a natural beauty, and I know at least one person who thinks so. Maybe the headlines jumped the gun, but has it crossed your mind that they aren't really that far off?"

"Dax and I are not together. And he definitely did not break up with Zola for me," Sonny persisted.

"Are you sure about that? Flings and casual affairs were more his style, but he was as moody as a sullen teenager when he thought you were mad at him. He begged me to get you to the dinner party, and Zola was long gone by the time he learned you would attend. Just think about it, Sonny. He doesn't really need you at his beck and call, but he insists that you're always by his side."

Sonny bit the corner of her lip. "Lillian, have you ever had an overzealous fan give you any trouble?"

"Sure. It kind of comes with the territory, but you learn to ignore it."

"But I—I mean someone who has scared you or become so invested in what you were doing that you ever felt threatened. Maybe like a stalker."

"Why? What's going on?"

Dax exited his trailer, and Sonny responded quickly, "Oh, nothing. Like I said, I'm just not used to all of the attention."

Dax locked eyes on the duo and started over.

"And, Sonny, you're wrong about another thing. Dax's eyes are like a laser pointer when you're in the room. It's as if you're the only thing he sees."

"I'm not so sure about all of that," Sonny said, embarrassed.

"Just my opinion, but, Sonny, he's one of the few good ones, even if he doesn't believe it himself."

ꕥꕥ

"What do you have planned for the rest of your evening? Besides hiding from unwanted media scrutiny?" Dax asked.

"I planned on visiting Vivian at her house. She was released from the hospital today, and although Sully is doing great, I know it must be one of the hardest things leaving your new baby at the hospital. She could probably use a friend."

Dax nodded. "At the risk of intruding on girl bonding time, do you mind if I drive you there. I want to make sure you're safe. I can even sit in another room if you want privacy."

"Don't be silly. You're welcome to join me."

"I am? I figured after this morning's events, you would want to get as far away from me as possible."

"This, too, shall pass, right?"

"Absolutely, but, Sonny, why the change of heart?"

"Let's just say I'm tired of letting this scumbag dictate our lives."

ග෧ග෧

"How is she?" Sonny asked Miles when he opened the door.

"Better than expected. I think it helps that we had a good report from Sully's nurses before we left. They said they were very hopeful that he would be home with us soon."

"That's great to hear."

"She's in the living room. Go on in."

Dax followed Miles into the kitchen to allow the women to talk.

"Sonny, I'm so glad you came by," Vivian said.

"How are you doing?" Sonny asked.

"I'm okay. Trust me, I've done my fair share of crying, but the nurses assured me my baby boy would join us at home before you know it, and it's been nice spending quality time with Drew. I'll be able to go to the hospital every day, so, hopefully, this will all be a distant memory before we know it."

Vivian sniffed, and Sonny embraced her compassionately. "You know I'm here if you need anything."

"I appreciate that so let's change the subject for a minute. I'm not so out of the loop that I haven't heard what is going on with you. When Miles was wheeling me out to the car, we passed by the gift shop, and I caught a glimpse of a magazine. I was surprised to see your face on the cover. What's going on?"

"Oh, that. Vivian, I don't even know where to begin. It was an innocent moment caught on camera that was leaked and now exploited to make headlines that are completely fabricated."

"I guess you'll have that in the world of celebrities, but how's that effecting you?"

"At first, I was completely mortified, but after gaining a little perspective, I realize that things could be much worse than gaining national attention. It'll all blow over, and that can't come soon enough, but it's just a picture." She shrugged her shoulders.

Vivian gave her a knowing look. "Is that all it is? There's nothing more to it than that? You two are attached at the hip. No feelings at all?"

Sonny sighed. "I would be lying if I said there haven't been moments shared between us, but that's all, just fleeting moments. I'm sure he'll grow bored of the challenge soon enough, and I don't intend to be the idiot who thought it was more than that."

"Have you heard anything more about your book?"

"Well, Hudson took it upon himself to send it to Lillian Grace, Dax's costar in the new movie. At first, I resented his boldness, but, honestly, it came from good intentions."

"And what did she have to say?"

"She loved it, said she had a good feeling about it. I'm not sure if her influence will get it anywhere, but at this point, it can't hurt, right?"

"Sonny, that's great. My fingers are crossed."

"Vivian, I have to talk to you about something. It's important, and you may be angry with me for not sharing it sooner, but please believe me when I say I just didn't want to draw any attention away from the miraculous birth of your son."

"I'm listening. What is it?"

"Dax has a stalker who may have had something to do with the accident that caused you to go into labor." Sonny started crying and put her face in her hands. "I was warned to stay away from him, and because of my connection to him, you all were hurt. This is all my fault," she sobbed miserably but forced herself to tell the whole story from the beginning.

By the time she had finished, both women were crying, and Sonny said, "I don't know how you'll ever forgive me. You named your son's middle name in honor of my book, but I don't deserve it. I don't blame you if you hate me," she hiccupped.

"If you're going to be angry with anyone, be angry with me," Dax said quietly. "It's not Sonny's fault."

Both women turned in his direction where he and Miles entered the room.

"Does Miles know?"

"Yes, he filled me in on everything, Sonny, and I'm angry, but not with you. I'm angry with the twisted psycho who did this. You couldn't have known."

Vivian agreed. "Sonny, you're one of my best friends. You were there for me after my divorce. You forget that we've been through crazy before and came out on the other side. I admit I had rather hoped we had experienced our fair share of if by now, but I know you to be one of the most loyal people I have ever met. I trust when you say you couldn't have known. But this person will pay for what they have done to my family, and that includes you. So where do we start?"

"We aren't sure exactly, but we believe the same person leaked the photo of us on the sidewalk, so they aren't finished with us yet."

"We've been spending so much time together to try and figure this out," Sonny said.

"I want you to bring me all of the letters, flowers included, any evidence at all," Miles said. "If not me, then I will have someone on it at the lab. We will nail them. Of that, I am sure."

Sonny hugged Vivian tight. "Thank you for showing me grace."

"Don't ever be afraid to talk to me."

Sonny wiped away tears. "I'm going to go wash my face, I'm a mess."

When Sonny left the room, Dax shifted uncomfortably. "I'm sorry I've brought this all on her and your family."

"Dax, you couldn't have predicted this, but I do insist that you take good care of her."

"You have my word. Most women I know would have run for the hills by now."

"Sonny's not most women," Vivian said.

"Trust me, I know."

Something about the way he said that prompted Vivian to push further. "You care for her."

"Lord help me, I do, but I'm afraid I'm not the easiest person and that I come with an awful lot of baggage. I'm making a mess of things."

"Give her credit. She's stronger than she gives herself credit for. She's an amazing, talented person who will inspire people with her gifts."

"I want to be a part of that, but I don't think she trusts me. She won't even let me read her story."

"She'll get there. Don't give up. If you really care, prove it to her."

"I'll try," Dax promised. "And I won't let her get hurt."

"Somehow, I believe you. Give me your email. If

you want to know Sonny, you must read her writing. That's where she truly puts it all out there."

"Why are you helping me so much? If you don't mind me asking."

"Because I want my friend to be happy, and she deserves that." Vivian looked over at Miles with feeling. "And because once upon a time, I too came with a lot of baggage, and I was lucky enough to have someone who didn't give up on me."

ꕥ

When Dax dropped Sonny off at her apartment, he asked her one more time. "Are you sure that you don't want me to stay? Safety in numbers, ya know?"

"Yes, but I'm sure. Hudson will be here so I won't be alone. I have a lot of writing to get caught up on."

"Okay. I understand, but do you want me to pick you up in the morning?"

"I can drive, Dax. There's no reason to back track. I'll be there bright and early."

Dax pushed his hands deeper into his pockets and rocked back and forth on his feels.

"What is it, Dax? Why the loss of words?"

"There's an award show. I'm sure you've seen it on my calendar. It's kind of a kick off to award-show season. I'm up for a nomination for *Sampson's Soldiers.*"

"Yes, I scheduled you for your tux fitting. Dax, it's this weekend. Don't tell me you're just now remembering."

"No, I remembered. I was kind of wondering if you would be my plus one?"

"Me? Really? You think that would be a good idea after all that has happened?"

"I was supposed to bring Zola, or rather she thought I would, anyway. So what do you say?"

"Oh, Dax, I don't know. Do you mind if I think about it? I don't have a dress. Isn't there a lot of preparation for these kinds of thing?"

"I can ask Lillian to help us with all of the girl things, and you don't need all of that preparation. You're beautiful just the way you are."

Sonny flushed. "You're doing it again."

"I mean every word of it. Just promise me you'll think about it."

He leaned forward and held his mouth right above hers. Her breath hitched.

"There might be cameras, Dax," she whispered.

"I don't care," he said gruffly. "Let them watch me kiss you."

His mouth claimed hers, and it was instant fire. She was tired of resisting, and she felt herself melt into his embrace. His hands tangled into her hair, and she titled her face up to his to deepen the kiss. He tasted good, and it felt good too. His tongue intertwined with hers, but the moment was brief when a car horn honked as it whizzed past, and teenagers whooped and hollered cat calls as they drove past.

Sonny pulled away, embarrassed, and he grabbed her hand to hold her there.

"So I'll see you in the morning?"

"Yes."

"Good, I can't wait. Be careful tonight, okay?"

"Bye."

He jogged down the stoop and, when she turned away, she couldn't help smiling like a school girl.

Dax hummed to himself all the way home. When he opened the door to his place, a voice greeted him.

"Hello, lover. Have you come to your senses yet?"

"Zola, what are you doing here?"

CHAPTER 20

Sonny arrived early at Dax's apartment, feeling rested and restored. She knocked on his door with somewhat nervous anticipation after the way they had left things the night before. She had butterflies as she waited for him to answer the door.

She smoothed her hair when she heard the click of the lock. When the door opened, a grin took over her face.

"Are you ready to—"

"Hello, Ms. Winslow," Zola said smugly as she planted herself in front of the opening.

"Zola, what are you doing here?" Sonny asked as she couldn't hide her surprise.

"I came in last night. I thought it would be a nice surprise for Dax. I figured he would be happy to see me, and I was right. I see he has kept you around. Dax always did feel sorry for the less fortunate."

Dax came into the foyer with a towel around his waist and another he used to dry off his hair. When he saw the two women, it took only a moment to read the scene taking place. The shock and hurt that registered across Sonny's face made his mouth go dry, and he dropped the towel from his head. "Zola, what are you doing back here?"

"Don't be silly, lover. You must have known I wasn't going to leave things unsettled between us. Last night when I saw you—"

"Last night?" Sonny interrupted.

"Sonny, this isn't what it looks like. She must have let herself in. She showed up unannounced."

"I cannot believe this," Sonny said, dejected.

"Well, believe it. Dax and I may have had a disagreement, but you don't just throw away a near-perfect relationship over a disagreement, right, Dax?"

"Shut up, Zola. You came here uninvited, and I made you leave. I had no idea she was here this morning, Sonny. She must have come in while I was in the shower. He looked from one woman to the other the women. "It's over, Zola, and I thought I made myself clear, but apparently, your delusions exceed my expectations of your mental health."

"I can't believe you're talking to me this way. I came here to help you. I saw the pictures released to the press, and I knew there must have been some mistake. There was no way you were involved with this charity case. So, I figured I could help you put the rumors to rest by getting back together with you, or denying we ever split in the first place. I figured a little appearance together at a certain award ceremony might be just what the media wants to see from us, the Hollywood 'it' couple."

"Now I know that you're delusional. I don't need or want to be seen with someone who treats people like crap. Sonny is so much more—"

"You don't have to go there, Dax. I can stand up for myself. This fantasy world you all live in is just too much for me. I'm over it." She turned and hurried away.

"Sonny, wait," Dax called after her.

"Do you really want pictures out there of you in a lover's quarrel with the waitress, chasing after her in nothing more than a towel?"

"Zola, Sonny is nobody's charity case. She's smart and talented, caring and kind. You may be a super model, but she lights up a room with her beauty, and that outshines your ugly behavior any day of the week."

Zola stuttered. "I—I can't believe this."

"Start believing. Now get the hell out."

"You'll regret this, Daxton, mark my words."

"Somehow I doubt that."

Zola stomped away, fuming.

A few minutes later, Dax was dressed and hurrying around the corner to the elevators. Sonny stood waiting with her arms crossed over her chest. She sniffed and pushed the button multiple times in an attempt to make it arrive faster.

"Sonny, I thought you left."

"Did you mean what you said? What you told Zola?"

"Every word. I never invited—"

She grabbed his face with her hands and planted her mouth on his. When she pulled away, she looked into his eyes. He was speechless. He took her in his arms, reconnecting his mouth with hers, and kissed her with fervor, which she returned with enthusiasm. He backed her against the elevator and pressed her against the door. Her skin felt the cool aluminum. She moaned as he caught her lower lips between his teeth. Dax kissed and nuzzled the soft skin of her neck and groaned.

"You're driving me crazy," he moaned.

A ding rang out and the elevator doors, opened causing them to fall backward.

Sonny laughed. "We better go. We're already late."

When they were on their way down, Dax said, "I'm sorry for how hateful Zola can be. What she said couldn't be farther from the truth."

"I'm sure that the moment I'm alone, I'll over analyze everything, but for now I'm trying to focus on the here and now."

"One day, when we look back on this, we'll laugh."

"Maybe, but let's not think about that."

"You, the planner, doesn't want to talk about the future?"

"Come on, Dax. You heard Zola. We don't belong together in each other's worlds."

"It works sometimes."

"When, Dax? When does it ever work?"

ꕥꕥ

Beverly stared out at the night sky from the balcony.

"What are you doing out here?" her maid of honor asked her.

"Just getting some fresh air. Go on, enjoy yourself."

"It's your rehearsal dinner, and you're barely socializing. Are you sure that you're okay?"

"Yes, I promise. Just a little nervous, I guess."

"That's to be expected. Tomorrow's going to be one of the most monumental days of your life."

"Well, when you put it like that, I have nothing to be nervous about at all, right?"

"Oh, come on. You're marrying one of the most eligible bachelors out there. He's great. It's going to be great."

"Yeah, he's great, on paper, but be honest, do you think he's great for me?"

"Of course I do. This is just crazy talk, Bev. But if he isn't, then you'll just divorce him. I mean, he's good enough for your first marriage. Right?"

She was kidding, of course, and it was enough to get Bev to smile.

"Now, are you coming back in to your party, or what?"

"Yeah, just give me a few minutes."

When Beverly was alone, she went back to staring out into the night, when a figure caught her eye. It was a man standing on the street corner looking up at the balcony with his hands in his pockets.

When she saw that it was Parker, her heart gave a little leap, but soon enough she was filled with remorse.

"Don't make me come up to get you. Are you coming down or what?"

Beverly looked through the glass doors and made sure that no one was looking her way. She went to the fire escape and tried to scurry down it as gracefully and quickly as possible.

"So what are you doing?"

She gaped at him. "What do you mean?"

"Come on, Beverly. You're going to go through with this? You're going to marry this guy. That's not what you want."

"How do you know what I want? You can't even determine that for yourself."

"Oh, I can't? I know that I want you."

"That's just because it's a challenge."

"You're a challenge all right, but it would be easier not to want you, trust me, but I can't do that."

"Why?"

"Because I love you, dammit!"

She stared at him in astonishment, and he grabbed her face intensely.

"I love you," he repeated. "Trust me. It comes as a surprise to me as well, but I do. I love you, and I'll never stop. I'll love you passionately the way you deserve. Don't go be with that guy. Be with me. I promise we will fight, but we'll love, and life will never be boring. What do you say?"

"You haven't known me long enough to love me."

"It may not have been that long, but I know that I'm the guy for you, and I know that you feel it too. We can't change it, so why fight it."

"Because it's wrong, and I can't. I'm sorry."

"Can't or won't?"

Tears spilled down her pretty porcelain cheeks. "I'm sorry."

She turned and left him standing in the streets. Her shoulders shook as her body was wracked with sobs when she reached a safe distance away from him. She took her time going back into the party.

"There she is. Now a toast to the happy couple."

She wiped away a lone tear as she tried to smile, hoping her guests would mistake them for happy tears.

ઌઌ

"So how's this movie going to end?" Sonny asked him.

"You've made it this far. We're almost finished so I guess you'll just have to wait and see."

"Not fair."

"What's fair? You don't want me to read your book."

"Eventually, you can read it when you buy it for yourself."

"I'll be one of the first in line, and I want an autographed copy and no impersonal message either. I want people to know that we were more than just acquaintances."

"You're awfully demanding. Speaking of being acquaintances, the movie is coming together ahead of schedule. So when you're done, you what? Just leave?"

Dax studied her face. "I'll be around for a little while longer. I'm sure they'll rewrite some scenes or have us redo them to better fit their criteria. You can't be rid of me that easily." He smiled and brushed a tendril of hair from her face. "Why? Anxious for me to go?"

She looked at him seriously. "Not quite."

His breathing slowed. "Not ready to give up the handsome paycheck."

"Something like that."

He walked closer to her slowly, afraid any sudden movements would ruin the moment. "Maybe you would miss me?"

"Maybe," she whispered. "I mean, I doubt it, but maybe."

"Yeah, me, too." His mouth crushed hungrily over hers and she reciprocated with the same intensity. "Sonny, I have to have you."

His hands were all over her body. His movements frenzied as he pulled her closer. He rubbed his manhood against her, and she felt his excitement.

Lightning flashed through her belly, and her hands squeezed the taut muscles in his back. A knock on his trailer door quickly drew them back to reality.

"Dax, we need to go over a line in the scene. Tell me you didn't already undress," his stage manager called through the door.

Dax looked down at his bulging erection and rubbed his forehead over hers in sexual frustration. "Apparently, I didn't undress fast enough," he groaned. "I will be there in a minute," he called out to his stage manager. "Sonny, tell me you're coming to LA with me." He kissed her full on the mouth. "Please, Sonny, just say yes. Let's get out of here."

CHAPTER 21

She still couldn't believe that she was boarding a private plane to fly half way across the country to attend a prestigious award ceremony for her current employer and occasional kissing buddy.

The minute they landed, she would be greeted by hair, makeup, and wardrobe. After the ceremony, they would be picked up by a limousine to go wherever their hearts desired for the night, and the next day it would be back on the plane to return home. If that wasn't jet setting, she didn't know what was.

On the way to the plane, she was still in denial that this was actually happening. Sonny went from barely making ends meet as a waitress, to getting a makeover and wearing designer gowns for a red-carpet event. What was this life? Whose world was she in because it certainly was not hers?

Dax read the apprehension on her face and smiled kindly while grabbing her hand. “We are in this together. Don’t be nervous.”

“I’m not,” she lied. “I do this all the time.”

She laughed and boarded the plane, determined to take in every last second because this was a once-in-a-lifetime opportunity.

“Is everyone prepared for takeoff, Mr. Knight?” the pilot asked.

“Yes, we are.”

Moments later, the small plane was airborne, and Sonny’s eyes never left the window.

“You can relax, you know,” Dax said.

“Not likely,” Sonny replied.

“Nervous flyer.”

“Maybe a little,” she admitted.

“There’s nothing to be afraid of.”

“Do you think they’ll follow us?”

Dax didn’t have to ask who she was referring to. “I’m not sure,” he answered honestly. “But I’m trying not to think about it. For the time being, we’re away from it all.”

“I know, but doesn’t it concern you that we’re no closer to figuring out who this person is?”

“Of course, it concerns me, but I choose to live in the moment with you.” He grabbed her hand. “I’m trying to let it go. I really am.”

“I know you are.”

It was a smooth ride with little turbulence, and they landed ahead of schedule.

A driver was waiting for them outside of the small runway, and Sonny was whisked away to a private hotel room for hair and makeup.

A rack of designer dresses, all in her size, were waiting for her to try them on.

"I'll see you before the show. Try to enjoy yourself."

Sonny was completely out of her element, and her nervousness must have been apparent.

"Come on, dear. We haven't got much time, and you have amazing cheekbones just waiting to be contoured." The stylist pushed Sonny down into a chair. "So how long have you and Mr. Knight been an item?"

"Oh, we're not together," Sonny corrected. "I'm just his stand-in assistant."

"Hmmm," the stylist mused. "If you say so, darling, but in my experience, a man doesn't look at a woman like that unless he has feelings."

Sonny turned red. "We're just friends."

"Whatever you say, but when he sees you after I'm through with you, he won't be able to resist himself. And, honey, you're going to have to stop blushing if I'm going to match your shade just right."

To Sonny's dismay, her blush deepened further.

 cscs

Dax knocked on her hotel room door, dressed in his tux and ready to go.

"Just a minute," she called out.

Dax stared at his shiny shoes while listening to the click of the door being unlocked. When it opened, he looked up in shock.

Sonny stood silently, fidgeting nervously. Neither of them said a word for what felt like an eternity.

"Well? Is it too much?" she asked.

"You take my breath away."

The look on his face was pure male appreciation as he admired her from head to toe.

"Dax, stop, you're embarrassing me."

"That's not my intention. It's just that, in all of my life, I've never seen a sight more beautiful."

Sonny's eyes met his in an intense stare. She shifted her weight from foot to foot. "You can't possibly mean that," she whispered.

"But I do," he said gruffly as she pulled her to him. "I'm not sure I'll be able to keep my promise to not touch you."

Heat rose through her body. "Dax," she pleaded.

"I know, we have to go, but I can't believe my luck that you're my date."

"Always the charmer," she murmured.

"I've never been more truthful," he promised seriously. "And tonight, you're all mine."

He grabbed her hand and ushered her toward the elevator. She was buzzed from being full of nerves and excitement, but nothing could top the endearing words she received from this man.

When they pulled up to the red carpet, her heart pounded in her chest. He sensed the uncomfortable anxiety and tried to put her at ease.

"Stay focused and keep moving forward. The flashes will nearly blind you, but I promise not to leave your side. Just hold my hand. We'll get through it together. You don't have to answer anything that you don't want to."

She nodded.

"Are you ready?"

She nodded again.

His eyes never left hers, and he kissed her hand tenderly. "Okay, we're ready," he told the driver. He turned back to her. "Take a deep breath and don't forget to smile."

The doors opened, and the roar of people screaming frantically filled their ears.

"Daxton Knight!"

"Over here. Dax, look this way."

"Who's your date tonight?"

Flashes went off and, as Dax had predicted, they nearly blinded her on the spot. Her legs felt weak, and she focused hard on not teetering in her heels. She wasn't nearly as practiced as the other starlets that she stood amongst.

Sonny had never felt more out of place in her life, and she felt her attention being pulled in a million directions. She could feel the panic rise in her chest, but just then she felt the pressure of Dax's hand on her lower back propelling her forward, and she remembered to smile graciously.

He ignored the screaming fans yelling both his name and the names of his characters. He stopped periodically for a posed photo op, and she tried to remain composed to stand up straight and suck in.

"You are doing great. We have one interview near the end. You can leave all the questions to me."

When they got to the end of the carpet, *E News!* had a station set up, and they waited until the well-known host was ready.

"And we are live from the red carpet with Daxton Knight, who is up for the award of best male lead in *Sampson's Soldiers.* Hello, Dax."

"Hello, it's a pleasure to be here this evening."

"It certainly is. Tell me, how did you feel when you got the news you were nominated for such a prestigious award?"

"Quite frankly, I thought it must be some kind of a mistake as the other nominees are also deserving. I can't tell you what an honor it is to be placed with such a talented group of men."

"*Sampson's Soldiers* was such a hit at the box office. Were you surprised by the warm reception it received from the audience?"

"You always hope that what you are working on will resonate with people, and when I read the script, I knew we had a good thing that I couldn't pass up, but I'm thrilled at how well it took off. I'm happy to be a part of it."

"This film has really catapulted your career. How does it feel to be America's 'it' boy?"

Dax laughed. "It's been a wild ride, of that you can be sure. I just hope I live up to everyone's expectations. I'm just a boy with a dream who still can't believe it's coming true."

"What a dream come true it is. You're working on a new film with actress Lillian Grace. How's that coming, and what can we expect?"

"The film is called *For Better or Worse* and, so far, it has definitely been better. Lillian is a wonderful actress and dear friend. *Sampson's Soldiers* was a pretty heavy subject matter. This film is more of a romantic comedy. You might shed some tears, but I wanted to try a different range and do a different kind of film."

"We are excited to see it. Can we expect more action films from you in the future?"

"I would love the opportunity. I enjoy working with stunt coordinators."

"Now on the more personal level, can we ask who your lovely lady is tonight?"

"This is Miss Sonny Winslow, she is my trusted assistant. And lovely she most certainly is."

"Reports have recently surfaced that you two may be an item. Can you confirm or deny if there's any truth to those rumors?"

Sonny's heart thudded in her chest.

"I can, but I won't." Dax smiled charmingly. "My personal life is just that, personal. Besides, I like to keep a certain air of mystique."

The host laughed. "Well, you're certainly succeeding. You two make a handsome duo, if I do say so myself."

"Thank you. Sonny's an author and her book, *Seize the Night*, will be available soon. She's a very gifted writer, and I encourage everyone to read it. She's going places."

Sonny's smile slipped for only a moment as the surprise registered on her features.

"I look forward to when it comes out."

"Thank you."

"I'll let you get to your seats and good luck. May we speak again?"

"I'll look forward to it."

Sonny kept her smile forcefully plastered on her made up face as they walked away. When they were out of earshot, she said, "Why did you do that?"

"Because I wanted to."

"I didn't ask you to."

"I know, which is even more reason why I wanted to."

"But you don't know if my writing is going anywhere or not. I'm surprised you knew the title."

"Oh, I know it's going somewhere. It's too good not to."

Sonny stared at him open mouthed.

"Don't be so surprised, I have connections you know."

"Lillian?"

"No, ironically. Someone close to you said if I wanted to get to know your heart, I would have to read your writing."

"Sounds like something Vivian would say."

Dax smiled.

"Vivian sent you my book?"

"Yes, and I couldn't put it down. You have a real gift."

"You read it already?"

Dax laughed. "What? Are you surprised I can read?"

"I just…" She was at a loss for words. "I just didn't know you were really that interested."

"Oh, I'm interested." He looked deep into her eyes. "It was an honor to know your story."

CHAPTER 22

After they rubbed elbows with people she had only seen on screen, they finally found their seats. Although she was overwhelmed by all the glitz and glamor, Sonny felt more comfortable after she had time to warm up.

She was surprised when Dax grabbed her hand and the look on her face must have said so.

"Enjoying yourself yet? That wasn't so bad was it?"

"No, it was a bit intimidating but not as bad as I expected it to be, I must admit."

"Good."

"Are you enjoying yourself?" she asked. "You must be nervous being nominated for such a huge award. It's a big deal."

"There is no guarantee I'll win."

"It would be a shame if you didn't. You're very deserving."

"How would you know? You haven't seen the movie."

Sonny looked at him sheepishly. "I may have rented the highly acclaimed film."

Dax looked at her in surprise. "You never said anything."

"Well, I needed to see what all of the hype was about."

"And?"

"It didn't disappoint. I was on the edge of my seat the whole time. It kept me awake that night."

The look on Dax's face showed he was pleased.

"Now don't go getting swollen ego on me," she warned.

"No, I was just thinking of other ways I could keep you up at night."

Sonny flushed.

"Because I already feel like I have won."

She looked at him inquisitively.

"Because you liked my movie."

She arched her brow. "I'm sure you were waiting on my opinion."

"Your opinion matters more than you know, Sonny."

He squeezed her hand, and they lapsed into silence as the lights dimmed and the show began.

The presenter's jokes were perfectly timed, the acts were entertaining, and the audience was rambunctious. It was more than what Sonny had even anticipated from the various award shows she had seen on television. She could feel the tension before they announced the winners and recipients shed tears and thanked their families. She was honored to be a part of such a special night and even more so that Dax wanted to share it with her.

It was inspiring to be in a room full of successful people following their dreams and witnessing their shining moment come to pass. She thought she might be more nervous than Dax was as he sat beside her calming applauding and sipping his beverage. He said very little, and she thought that maybe the anticipation was to blame. But she resisted the urge to comment on it.

The night was nearing the end, as his category was one of the last to be called out. Waiting was torture, and she couldn't imagine what he must be feeling.

Finally, after another music act finished their hit song, two well-known presenters took the stage. Dax grabbed her hand, and she squeezed his reassuringly.

She glanced over and studied his face. Outward appearances could be deceiving as he looked cool as a cucumber, but his pulse ticked underneath the hand she had placed on his arm.

All the nonsense aside, Dax was a very talented actor who worked hard at his craft. He was a rising star and deserved to be recognized, but even believing he had it in the bag, she knew he was up against some big names that were established in the business. To be the best, you had to go up against the best. Knowing where he came from made her want it for him all the more.

He met her eyes and, for a moment, she saw the small, younger boy, who was vulnerable and lost, trying to find his way. The boy whose own insecurities developed from his mother's actions. He sought approval then and needed it still to feel validated. He was a great actor, but even he couldn't mask the feelings of inner turmoil he felt now.

"Dax," she whispered. "No matter what happens, you're wonderful at what you do, and no award can give or take away your talent. You have a long career ahead of you with countless opportunities. I just want you to know that you should be proud of how far you have come and that, although I believe you're going to hear your name, it doesn't define who you are. You're an amazing man and thank you for letting me share this important moment with you." She squeezed his hand sincerely.

Tears filled his eyes. "Thank you, Sonny, and I want you to know that, no matter what happens or how my mood fluctuates, I had a really great time tonight, and there's no one else I would rather be with tonight. You inspire me to be a better man."

They stared hard into each other's eyes, and she gulped at the lump that formed in her throat. She turned her attention back to the stage and squeezed his hand.

"And the winner for this year's best male lead is…"

It seemed to take forever for the pretty female to open the envelope, and Sonny willed her to hurry up. She closed her eyes and held her breath.

"Daxton Knight for *Sampson's Soldiers!"*

Sonny let out her breath, and the crowd erupted into applause. She turned excitedly to Dax. He sat planted in his seat.

"Dax, it's you. You won." She hugged him. "You did it. I'm so proud of you."

His expression was one of complete surprise. "I didn't prepare a speech," he said. "I didn't want to jinx myself."

She smiled broadly. "Go, Dax, accept your award, and do what you do best. Wing it."

The people around them slapped him on the back and yelled out their congratulations. He started to walk up and turned at the last second to plant a hearty kiss on her mouth.

She was stunned as all the cameras were focused on the man of the hour and he strutted confidently toward the stage.

Her eyes welled up as she watched him hug the presenters and accept his award. She clasped her hands over her mouth as he positioned himself in front of the mic, preparing to give his acceptance speech.

The tears flowed freely down her face as she beamed with pride. He thanked his fellow actors who he worked alongside of and the nominees for inspiring him and pushing him to work hard to be great.

Dax's voice quivered as he choked back emotion when he thanked the teachers that took a chance on him. "Especially one in particular who took the time to believe in me, She knows who she is. She pushed me to see something in myself that she saw long before I did. To that woman, I thank you. Your faith in me means more than you will ever know. I also want to thank another very special woman. In a short amount of time, she has not only managed to inspire me, she has encouraged me and challenged me to be a better man. So thank you for not only organizing my work schedule but also getting me back on track with my life. Thank you for making me realize what's important and what I want to strive for. This award is a huge honor, and I don't accept it lightly. Thank you all. This night will go down in the books as one of the most memorable nights of my life, and I encourage everyone to seize the night. You only live once. Thank you."

He held the award and gave it a fist pump in the air as the crowd applauded. He smiled a charming smile, and she swore she could see the glint in his eyes from where she sat. That smile was dangerous, but full of promise, and it warned her from head to toe like the after effects of a buzz from liquor filling your veins, leaving you flushed and feverish, caution being thrown to the wind. Hearing him mention her so thoughtfully and sincerely pulled at something down deep, and it was more than just an eager sex drive. Whatever it was left her feeling giddy with excitement and the unspoken promise of what could be in store for them.

She felt like a school girl, imagining all of the things they would do and replaying his flirtations and countless innuendos in her mind. Maybe it was time she completely let go of her inhibitions and just enjoyed herself. She was eager for him to return, but she knew that he was celebrating and being interviewed backstage. Before she knew it, the final act was ending, and Daxton still had not made it back.

Great, she thought. Now she would have to finagle her way back stage and search for him amongst all the other famous and infamous faces. This shouldn't be awkward at all.

"Sonny, I've been looking for you," Lillian called. "Dax told me to come find you and lead you back stage."

"Lillian, you have no idea how nice it is to see a familiar face. Well, I mean an actual familiar face, like one that I have talked to. This can be a little overwhelming."

"Tell me about it. I still find it nerve wracking. Come on, he's just right back here."

Sonny followed Lillian backstage, and people buzzed around them jam packed, elbow to elbow. The pandemonium was both overwhelming and exciting. It was a blur of designer duds, champagne, and noise, cameras, interviews, and more noise. Across the expanse of commotion, Dax's eyes met with Sonny's. The magnitude of intensity that Dax's gaze held took Sonny's breath away.

Everyone who filled the room faded away. It was as if they all disappeared and all that mattered was the emotion that was portrayed in that one look. It was all for her. He only had eyes for her.

Her face filled with heat, and her eyes fluttered shyly under his smoldering stare. With one word, he excused himself from the interview he was in the middle of giving.

Sonny's eyes never left his as he walked toward her. Lillian continued babbling in her ear, oblivious to the moment of clarity and passion transforming right in front of her. It wasn't until Dax was almost directly in front of them that Lillian became aware of the electricity that filled the air. It almost reached out and zapped her, if she threated to enter the force field that charged between Dax and Sonny.

"I can take a hint when I'm being ignored. Congratulations, Dax, on your much-deserved win. I was going to invite you out for drinks, but I think I'll retract the offer. You two would only serve to make a single gal even more lonely."

Sonny never broke eye contact with Dax, but said, "If you need the company."

"No, thanks, you might outshine even me in that dress. I've got to tell my stylist to stop doing too good of a job." Lillian smiled. "No, I'm going to excuse myself to go find people who aren't completely self-absorbed."

Dax laughed as his co-star walked away. "You ready to get out of here?"

His face held a look of anticipative hopefulness that took on a boyish quality.

"Don't you want to go out to celebrate your big win?"

His light-hearted smiled took on one of earnestness. "Sonny, this is exactly what I want to be doing, I promise you."

She lowered her lashes and whispered, "Okay, let's go."

ဖဖ

He watched as Dax and Sonny made their way to the exit, hand in hand, unaware of the flock of people still congregating in the theater. Dax whispered something inaudible into Sonny's ear, and she giggled like a love-struck teenager.

It was sickening the way they paraded in front of everyone, completely ignoring all the warnings they had been given. It was time to show them they weren't mess-ing with an amateur. Sonny had not heeded his advice, so if she was caught in the crossfires that was her own problem. Who did she think she was, anyway? Fucking Cinderella?"

"That's not the way the real world works, Sonny, and I'm done feeling sorry for you. I thought you were a nice girl, another one of Dax's victims, but it turns out you're no better than he is, you naïve, stupid girl. You'll learn soon enough, and Daxton is going to get what's coming to him."

He smiled underneath the mask, and he could taste the salt as sweat pooled beneath the warm material, stinging his eyes. He had been patient enough. Dax couldn't walk away with an award and the girl. That was just too much to bear, so he hunkered down and waited in the alley where he had a clear view of his target.

His body itched with anticipation, and his pulse drummed in his ears. He could barely contain his excitement as he watched them draw closer. He tried to school his breathing to calm himself down when a woman stopped the couple. She appeared angry. His interest peaked, he leaned forward in an attempt to better hear their conversation.

"Zola, what do you want?" Dax said.

"I can't believe you brought her here. It really shows you had no feelings for me at all. You have sunk to an all-time low."

"No, Zola. I finally dug myself out of the low pit I was in when I was with you."

"How can you treat me as if I'm dispensable?"

"How can you talk about Sonny as if she's a piece of garbage I found on the street? She's a wonderful person, but you would never know that because you don't associate with people below your pay grade. That's all that matters to you."

"Just because I like to associate myself with people who are in the same class does not make me evil, Daxton. Besides, you're too blind to see she's using you to promote her book."

"I chose to promote her work because she's articulate and one of the most-talented people I have come across. She has a lot more skill than trying on clothes and taking a decent selfie. Besides, you and I obviously have very different views on what evil is. Now leave us alone. You're drunk and going to say or do something you'll regret. Don't make a scene, Zola. The media isn't very forgiving. Come on, Sonny."

They started to walk away, leaving Zola screeching obscenities behind them.

He was cut off from his eavesdropping when a voice behind him said, "Hey, man. Can I bum a smoke?"

He turned slowly to see a homeless man that had left his retreat beside a dumpster. "Not now," he growled.

"Hey, man, why you wearing a mask? You planning on robbing somebody?"

"None of your damn business."

"Well, see, it kind of is. I took up residency here because they throw out some good food here. I may not have much, but I eat like a king. I don't want no trouble."

"Take a hike and go back to your dumpster diving," he said as he tried to shove past the man.

But the bum was faster than he anticipated and shoved him against the brick wall so hard he momentarily saw stars. When he cleared his head, the man was trying to remove the mask.

He pushed back out of sheer self-preservation, and the homeless man fell to the ground. He looked back to the street, but Sonny and Dax had moved on.

"You screwed up everything," he screamed as he took off running.

"That's right. Go, and don't come back into my territory again. You hear me?"

The words feel on deaf ears as the masked man sprinted down the block.

CHAPTER 23

Daxton Knight," a voice called out. "Wait a minute, man, hold up. I may have some important information for you."

Dax blew out a sigh of exasperation. "What now?"

"I know you must get stopped a lot, but I think I might have something you want to hear."

When Dax turned around, he saw a dirty man in tattered clothes. He could smell the stench from where he was standing and, although he tried to remain impassive, his face must have registered his disgust.

That didn't stop the man from continuing to approach them. Dax stepped in front of Sonny to barricade her from the unknown destitute.

The man held up his hands in mock surrender. "I know I must look a sight, especially to folk like you, but I mean no harm."

When Dax didn't see a weapon, he let his guard down, but only slightly.

"Hey, look, man, I live in the alley behind the theater. I know it ain't much, and I'm just a street rat to you, but I've got one of the better digs in the city, and I would like to keep it that way."

"What does that have to do with me?" Dax asked cautiously.

"Well, you see, I was waiting in the shadows by the dumpster for yawl's leftovers, filet mignon, right?"

The drifter smiled a toothless grin and, at the same time Dax silently wondered how he could chew a hunk of meat at all, Sonny's heart went out to him. She patted Dax's back as if silently telling him to be kind.

"Yes, it was a surf and turf. You'll really enjoy it."

"Yeah, that's why I got the best spot in town," the vagabond said as if that explained his situation completely.

Dax nodded as if he completely understood, although he was still wondering what this had to do with him.

"Anyway, tonight there was another man trying to share my spot. I didn't say anything at first, as I figured there would be plenty of food for us both to feast on and occasionally I do like the company."

Dax nodded again.

"But the dude was odd and obviously spying on somebody, so minding my own, I left him to it. Maybe an ex-girlfriend, you know, what have you? None of my business. But then I saw you getting into it with that girl. She's on all the covers of the magazines."

"Yes, Zola Wallace."

"Yeah, she's the one, pretty thang, but she has a mouth on her."

Dax snorted in agreement. "You can say that."

"Well, the dude got all jumpy watching you two go at it. I could hear him breathing all heavy, and he kept reaching for his pocket. So I nonchalantly asked him for a smoke to get a better read on the guy. When he turned around, I saw he was wearing a ski mask, and in this heat wave I knew he was planning something dirty."

"What did he do when he when you interrupted him?" Sonny asked, finding her voice.

"Well, miss, he didn't take too kindly to it. Pardon my language, but he was fucking pissed. I warned him not to start no trouble, but he shoved me and told me to stay out of it. Something about him didn't sit right with me."

"So what did you do?"

The man smiled, revealing some rotten teeth that had yet to fall out. "I knocked him up pretty good, but when I tried to take off the mask, he pushed me to the ground and took off. As soon as I regained my bearings, I took off to find you."

"And, once again, why do you think this has something to do with me?"

"Because he was mumbling to himself like a damn

lunatic. He said I screwed everything up, but Daxton Knight would get his."

Sonny's stomach dropped out from underneath her.

"That's you, right? You're the actor, Daxton Knight?"

"Yeah," Dax said. "It's me."

"Thought so. Your name Sonny?"

Sonny let out an audible gasp.

"He mumbled something with your name too. Real crazy ass if you ask me. Just thought you should know that Zola girl may not be the only one who has it in for you tonight."

"Thanks for the warning, man," Dax said sincerely. "Why did you take the initiative to come tell me?"

"Brothers gotta stick together dog. You played in that movie *Sampson's Soldiers* about the war, right? Shot up by your own men."

"Yeah. You've seen it?" Dax asked surprised.

The impoverished man smiled sheepishly. "Sometimes I sneak in to watch some of the films, but don't tell anyone. Yours was one of my favorites. I served in the in the war, but some shit went down. I was discharged, and now don't got nowhere to go."

"I'm sorry," Dax said sincerely.

"Don't pity me, Knight. I'll be eating some steak and lobster tonight."

"I hope you enjoy it. What was your name?"

"Terrell Williams, but my friends used to call me TW."

"TW, it was nice to meet you. Thanks for having my six." Dax reached into his wallet and pulled out a few hundred dollar bills. "I'd give you more, but it's all I got on me."

"Thanks, dog, you didn't have to do that. That's not why I told you, but you're a good dude."

"I know, you told me because you're a good dude too." Dax shook his hand. "And you may have saved our lives."

"Anytime, and, Knight, stop by anytime you're in the area. We can swap stories."

"I'll do that, TW. Stay safe, my man, and thank you."

ᘓᘓ

"Who the hell does he think he is?" Zola cried. "No one talks to me like that. He chose to take her, over me. I never thought he would follow through with it, ya know?" She hiccupped and wiped her nose with the back of her hand. "I've never been so embarrassed."

"I'm sure that it'll all work out Ms. Wallace," her driver said.

"Do you think so? What was your name again?"

"Jimmy."

"One day, I'll remember that, I swear."

"Somehow I doubt that," Jimmy said underneath his breath.

"What did you just say?"

Jimmy was saved by the ring tone as her phone went off.

"Hello."

"Ms. Wallace?"

"Yes, who's this?"

"Someone who wants to see Daxton Knight suffer."

"Yeah, you better get in line," Zola huffed.

"I was thinking that two heads might be better than one."

"You're saying you want to work together to bring Dax down?"

"Now you're catching on," he purred.

❧❧

"Maybe we shouldn't do this tonight," Sonny said.

Dax raised an eyebrow. "Do what?"

"Come on. You deserve to celebrate. Tonight is a big night for your career, but running into Zola, and being her punching bag yet again, has a way of putting a damper on the excitement for the evening."

"This has nothing to do with TW telling us about the masked mystery man? Besides, you should know by now not to let anything that Zola says get to you. I have no respect left for her and, if I had to guess, tomorrow she won't have any for herself either. Are you really going to let a sloppy drunk ruin the rest of our evening?"

"Look I do know better, and I'm trying to have thicker skin, but a girl can only take so much. She delivers the lowest blows every time. She loves to hit you where it hurts. I'm sure she's not the only one who thinks we don't belong together. Someone has it in for us, Dax, you in particular. If Zola hadn't come to unleash her wrath, we might have experienced something or someone much worse and seeking vengeance. My mind just can't take any more of this."

"I'll respect your decision either way. I'm not happy about it, and more than a little disappointed, but I want you to know that tonight was one of the best nights of my life, and I'm glad I had you to share it with. I refuse to let any of the other bogus absurdities tarnish my memory of this night."

They stopped at the door of her hotel room.

"You look beautiful tonight, and I'll be right next door if you need anything." He reached out to her and gently kissed the top of her head, before opening the door for her.

"Congratulations, Dax."

He smiled blandly. "I was looking forward to another award-winning performance tonight, but looks like I've been shot down again."

He didn't wait for a reply as he promptly retreated to his room and shut the door with a loud click.

She stood there for a while, looking at the door to his room, contemplating all of the chain of events that had taken place in the course of a day. It had really been a long one, including travel and primp time. Her body was exhausted, but when she finally shut the door and lay on the bed, her mind would not stop racing.

Dax was right next door. One conjoining door separated them. Everything would be fine. At least that was what she kept repeating to herself.

CHAPTER 24

Dax tossed and turned. He was too keyed up. Even raiding the mini bar hadn't helped. He used his shirt tail to pop off the bottle cap to his Budweiser and drew a long swig from the neck.

This was ridiculous. Why the hell was he not ordering room service and sipping a celebratory glass of champagne in between rounds of rolling around with a naked Sonny? He should have been sliding that dress off of her smooth skin and then he would—

"Screw this." He jumped up and strode across the room, slopping his beer over the brim as he went. "Sonny." He banged on the conjoining door. "Sonny, open up. I don't care what anyone else thinks. We shouldn't be alone. We should be together. Come on, open up."

He started to pound on the door again and rolled his forehead from side to side against the smooth wood.

Without warning the door opened abruptly, causing Dax to stumble forward.

"Shit," he swore when he stubbed his toe.

"Are you okay?" Sonny asked with mild humor filling her voice.

"You weren't sleeping?"

"No, I didn't even try. There's way too much going on in my head. I'm just so tired of thinking."

"Then stop," he growled. "Stop thinking and just be. Be with me."

His voice was raw with need, and the throaty sound caused an ache low in her belly.

His eyes held heat. "You didn't change out of your dress."

She lowered her lashes. "No, I didn't."

"Good, that's my job," he whispered. He titled her face up toward him, and his lips hovered above hers. "Look at me when I tell you that I want you."

She gasped, and he kissed the breath out of her. When his lips met hers, passion erupted, and a fire ignited. She whimpered quietly at the intensity of emotion that washed over her.

He cradled her with both hands and deepened the kiss with such vigor he left her breathless.

"Wait, Dax."

"I can't." He nibbled her neck and nipped her earlobe. "I have to have you, Sonny. I need you. This dress was beautiful, but it's got to go. I want to see you, feel you."

His mouth met hers again, and she responded hungrily. Her tongue melted against his, and he grunted his gratitude.

He found the tiny zipper, and his fingers fumbled with it clumsily. He sighed in frustration, and she grinned mischievously.

Sonny turned around slowly, and he unclasped the small hook and slowly unzipped the thin material all the way down to the slight feminine curve of her lower back. She shivered as her skin was exposed and his fingers brushed over her body.

"You feel so good." He kissed the back of her neck. "And you taste good too," he said as he traced patterns with his tongue.

"You're driving me crazy," she moaned.

Daxton lowered the straps, and she held the dress tight to her front.

"Don't ask me to stop now. Please," he groaned.

"I don't want you to."

"Then what's the problem?"

Sonny hung her head.

"Talk to me, Sonny."

"It's just that your last girlfriend was a super model. Excuse me, but that's a little intimidating."

He smiled a small grin and spun her around to meet her eyes. "You." He held her gaze and bent his head to kiss her again. "You're amazing, Sonny, inside and out. I've never wanted something as much as I want you tonight."

"That means a lot coming from a man who was just honored with a huge award," she said gruffly.

"Exactly. That should tell you something. Now, if you don't mind, I would like to keep admiring your beautiful body."

He pried her fingers away from the dress, and it slid to the floor slowly.

Appreciation was visible in the way his eyes dilated and darkened as they clouded over.

"Baby, there's nothing that could turn me on more than the sight of you."

His mouth crushed down on hers and his hands molded over her body, settling on her tight round bottom and pressing her hard against him so that she could feel just how excited he was. The hard bulge was undeniable and made her flush, slightly embarrassed, but also pleased with the level at which he was turned on by her.

His mouth was hot and wet on her skin. One hand kneaded her breast and tweaked her nipple hard, causing her to shriek from surprise and pleasurable pain.

She reached up and ran her fingers through his hair, returning his caresses with the same zeal, matching his enthusiasm tenfold. In a moment of confidence, she reached to the hard appendage below his waistline and rubbed the bulb between her fingers.

Dax was astonished at the momentary act of courage. He pulled back from the kiss and met her eyes. He saw a flicker of self-doubt pass over her face, and he wanted to erase it.

"Is this okay?" she asked timidly.

"Okay? Sonny, it's more than okay. You might want to stop." He gave her a pained expression. "But only if you don't want this night to end prematurely."

She abruptly stopped massaging his manhood.

"Oh, that got your attention. I was slightly exaggerating. Besides," he whispered. "I plan to make love to your body all night long."

She smiled and continued caressing.

"You haven't had much practice, have you?" he asked tenderly.

Her head snapped up. "Is it that apparent?"

He brushed her cheek sweetly. "No, I just mean you're a good girl, aren't you? You have no need to second guess yourself, but the fact that you do shows you don't slip under the sheets with just anyone or take sex lightly. You only sleep with someone you care about."

"Yeah, so?" she said defensively. "Is it a disappointment that I'm not some easy lay who probably has all the latest moves out of Kama Sutra?"

"Not at all. It's hot as hell and, at the risk of sounding arrogant, it makes me feel considerably significant." He nuzzled her bosom. "And I have got to say that feels pretty damn good."

He tried to be more gentle and to move slowly and take his time, but the quiet moans she made in his ear were enough to drive him mad. His fingers found their way to her lace panties, and he could feel that she was ready. He lost all resolve when her wet center tightened around his fingers, and he quickly pushed the panties down. He struggled to remove his pants in his haste to rejoin her body.

"I wanted to take my time, but dammit, Sonny. I have to have you."

They fell onto the bed, and he entered her in one swift motion. He filled her completely, and she gasped, calling out his name. Dax tried in vain to slow down, but the attempt was futile.

"You feel too good," he breathed. He moved in and out of her, and she wrapped her legs around him tilting her hips to allow him to penetrate deeper.

She climbed higher and grabbed a fistful of the bed-sheets. Dax covered her hand with his and interlaced their fingers. He watched her arch her head back as she went over the brink into delirium.

She bit her lip, and a moan escaped her swollen mouth as her pulse visibly ticked in the delicate skin of her neck. Watching the beautiful sight of her climax and feeling her tighten around him was enough to push him over the edge.

Losing all control, he emptied into her, drowning in a sea of pleasure.

ᴄᴐᴄᴐ

"That tickles," Sonny murmured as Dax traced lazy shapes across her exposed hip.

He kissed her shoulder and drew her closer to him. "So tell me. How is it that a woman like you hasn't been swooped up by some lucky bastard?"

"Come on, Dax. It's not as if I'm a virginal school girl, if that's what you're getting at. I've been with other men, granted not many, but you didn't deflower me and take away my innocence."

"It may not be many, but enough that it makes me insanely jealous."

She laughed. "Coming from a man who probably can't wash the bed sheets fast enough between lovers."

"Hey, now. Admittedly, I haven't always made the best choices, but you took the time to think about quality versus quantity."

"Yeah." She rolled over on her stomach. "And where are they now? It worked out really well for me. Now, I'm just another notch on Daxton Knight's bed post. Besides, I wanted to focus on my writing."

"Sonny." He waited until she met his eyes. "You are not another notch. You mean something to me. Besides, it's I who should feel honored to be intimate with the talented up and coming author."

She rolled her eyes but was pleased to hear his complimentary praises.

"In all seriousness, Sonny, you're a very talented writer. Do you guard your heart so closely because of your father? You realize how quickly things can be taken away? *Seize the Night* is a true story, right?"

"Yes. How did you know?" she asked, surprised.

"Lucky guess. It explains a lot. Your father died the same night you were born? Your mother went into labor after a car accident, and your father was air lifted to the hospital."

Tears pooled in her eyes. "They worked tirelessly, but couldn't save him. My mother's happiest day was also the worst. For all intents and purposes, the man my mother later married is my father, and I couldn't love him any more than if we shared the same DNA."

"He was a flight nurse who worked on your father that night, right?"

"Yes, he promised my mom that he would do everything he could to save him before they whisked him away, and, before my father completely lost consciousness, he promised him that he would make sure that my mom and I were okay. Of course, it didn't happen right away, but Ace couldn't shake the promise he made a dying man, so he started coming around to help my mom out. Eventually a love grew and, out of tragedy, they've created a beautiful life together. He stepped up and became a father to me, and I'll forever be grateful. They have a beautiful love story, and it taught me substance over simplistic ideals of overabundance. Sometimes less is more, you know?"

He rubbed his hand over her cheek. "I'm starting to realize."

She kissed his palm of his hand.

"So would I seem greedy if, in the case of you, I say I want more? You can't lie next to me naked and look at me like that without getting my blood pumping."

Just then there was a knock on the door.

"Hold that thought, Romeo. Room service is here." She threw on a robe. "You're in no condition to answer the door like that. You would no doubt embarrass us both."

She signed for the food and handed the man a generous tip. Rolling the cart of food toward the bed, she handed Dax his drink.

She paused when she saw the paper underneath the saucer.

"What is it, Sonny?"

"It's a note," she said flatly. "It says, 'You can't escape me. I will always find you. XOXO.'"

CHAPTER 25

"So how's my best friend the jet setter, doing?" Vivian squealed when she opened the door.

"I'm fine. The bigger question is how's my honorary nephew doing? Any word on when that beautiful baby's coming home?"

Vivian averted her gaze from meeting Sonny's.

"Oh, no, what is it, Viv? Is Sully okay?"

"Well, you'll just have to go into the nursery and see for yourself." Vivian's eyes sparkled.

"Wait, what? He came home? When? Vivian, I'm so happy." Tears flooded her eyes, and she wrapped Vivian in an excited bear hug. "It's so soon. They said they anticipated him staying in longer. What made them change their mind?"

"We were as shocked as you are, but that's the way it works in the NICU. Once they get over the hump, and they move to the side of the feeders and the growers, things can move very quickly. I questioned if they knew what they were doing by sending this baby home with us, and, as a precaution, they gave us a heart rate monitor. It's a band that goes around his tiny little chest, and it will alarm us if his heart rate drops or goes too high, or if he goes any length of time without breathing. On one hand that petrifies me, but on the other, it's nice to be re-assured that I'll be made aware if anything were to go wrong."

Sonny squeezed her friend's hands. "But it won't. I just know that everything will be perfect. Now let me see this miracle baby."

Vivian led Sonny over to the little bassinet.

"You can wake him. It's about feeding time, and we're trying to keep him on the same schedule that he was on at the hospital."

Sonny reached in, careful of the chords that poked out under the swaddled blankets. Sully stretched and tried to wriggle his little arms out of his tight position.

"Hey there, little man," Sonny cooed to him. "You really are handsome, you little miracle you. Now don't scare your mommy and daddy by making your monitor go off, you hear me? You'll be out of that thing before you know it. Now your mommy has to feed you so that you keep growing big and strong."

Sonny passed him over to his mama who gently nuz-zled him to wake him up enough to nurse. It was beautiful watching him suckle and feed from his mother, completely vulnerable and dependent on the one person who loved him more than anyone else on the planet.

Vivian looked up from her newborn son to see Sonny sniffling softly.

"Are you okay?"

"Yes, I'm just so happy and relieved."

"Come on, Sonny, what else is going on? How was your trip?"

"It was good. Dax won." She shrugged her shoulders.

"That's all I get? I knew that much from watching television. I also know that he gave a shout out to your book. That shows he believes in you, almost as much as I do."

"He read it. I asked him how he got the manuscript, and he wouldn't reveal his source, but I happen to know that I haven't trusted many with a copy."

Vivian smiled sheepishly. "What was his response to your beautifully written story?"

"He guessed that it was based on true life events."

"And?"

"And he said he believes in me and my writing."

Vivian smiled pleased. "Then I will not apologize for the fact that I may or may not have made sure your manuscript got into his hands."

"His words were, 'Someone close to you said that if I wanted to get to know the real you, I would have to read your writing.' It sounded like something you would say," Sonny said ruefully.

"Yeah, well. I plead the fifth, but I'm sure that person is very wise and also knows that Daxton Knight has developed serious feelings for you. That person would never have shared your work unless she knew that to be true."

Sonny contemplated Vivian's words. "He enjoys spending time with me, but once the movie's over, I'm sure he'll find a different girl in the next city. It's what he does."

"Maybe that's what he used to do. That's what he did before he met you. And you care about him too. I can see it in your eyes."

"He's infuriating, completely self-absorbed, unorganized, and uses his charm to supersede all of it."

"And that charm has worked its way right into your heart."

"Just because you're all in love and feeling sentimental over the motherhood stuff, doesn't mean you can go diving into my heart, or my head, for that matter. I promise you, it'll just confuse you."

"Well, that's what friends are for, to help you untangle all of the knots. So let me help you."

"It's obvious we've just bonded over being terrorized by his stalker, and have I mentioned he has a crazy ex-girlfriend? She just appears out of nowhere to constantly remind Dax that I'm not in their social circle. That's a lot to take on and sort out."

"Yes, it is, but the good things in your life are worth it, and I hate to say it, but it doesn't always come easy. Take me for example, I'm married to the man of my dreams with two beautiful kids and a successful business, and you and I both know that did not come easy by any means, but I wouldn't change it for the world. I wouldn't have all the people and things I love without a few trials and tribulations."

"How are you so wise, and usually right?"

"Experience. Now start from the beginning, and we'll sort this all out."

"It's going to take a while."

"I've got nothing better to do than listen and hold my beautiful baby boy."

ఌఌ

"Just a second," Dax yelled out. He wrapped a towel around his waist on the way to the door. He peeked through the peephole and blew out a long breath, along with a string of curse words, before flinging the door open. "Zola. You've got to stop dropping by like this."

"Well, hello to you too," she pouted.

"You understand that we're over, right? As in, no longer together. It's time for us to move on and see other people." Dax emphasized this with dramatic hand movements.

"Like moving on with Sonny? You really do like her?"

"Yes, I really do like her, but even if she wasn't in the picture, you and I would not be together."

She reached out and grazed his arm with her fingertips. "I find that a little hard to believe."

Dax jerked back.

"Relax, you used to enjoy my touch, now you act as if you've been scorched by Satan himself. You must really hate me."

Tears filled her eyes, and she bit her lip. For the first time, Dax saw Zola show real emotion.

"I don't hate you, Zola."

"You don't?" she asked skeptically.

"No, I feel sorry for you. Somewhere along your road to success, you have hardened yourself and become cold. I know that there's a human being with feelings in there somewhere, but your hateful behavior as of late has made it hard to believe. I know that behind all of that false confidence and show of bravado, or better-than-thou attitude, is just an insecure girl who was afraid she wouldn't catch her big break. Maybe people treated you that way, and now that you're in the big leagues you're paying the wrong kind of acts forward, but you've got to be better than that. Otherwise, you're never going to be truly happy—or find true love, for that matter."

"Look at you, that's the pot calling the kettle black, wouldn't you say?"

"I'm working on it, Zola. I'm trying to better myself, admittedly, I'm still a work in progress, but that's why I'm distancing myself from negative people."

"People like me?" she sniffed.

"Yes," Dax confirmed. "But if it makes you feel better, you aren't the only one."

"I know, Daxton, that I haven't been myself, in quite some time, but I didn't come here today to start any trouble. I came here to warn you."

Dax's heart stopped, and his once-warm skin from his shower was now chilled with chicken skin as his hair stood on end. "Warn me about what?" He forced the words out of his mouth.

"The night of the awards ceremony something happened. After I went off on you and Sonny, I received a phone call—"

"From who?" Dax interrupted.

"I don't know. If I did, I would have lead with that. Keep in mind that I was intoxicated so my memory's a little hazy."

"Dammit, try to remember. This is important." He raised his voice.

"Don't yell at me. Obviously, I know it's important, or I wouldn't be here," Zola snapped.

"Okay, go on. I'm sorry. Please continue." He motioned for her to keep talking and hung his head so that he could hide his irritation.

"The caller was a man who said he wanted to see you suffer. He made reference to us working together to bring you down. At first, I played into it—I was pissed and hurt, so wipe that judgmental look off of your face. The longer I talked to him, the more my gut told me that this man's dangerous, and he has an ax to grind. It was definitely more revenge than I was willing to get involved with. Dax, I'm sorry about the way I have behaved, but this guy, I think he could inflict some real harm. I wish I could give you more information, but once he knew I wasn't on board, he said he should have known he couldn't take a bitch like me seriously. Or at least it was something like that because like I said it was a little—"

Dax rubbed his hands over his face in frustration. "Hazy, yeah I got that part."

"I wanted to warn you because if something happened to you, and I could have prevented it, I would never forgive myself. I really do care about you."

She wrapped her arms around his neck seductively.

Dax grabbed her hands to unclasp them.

"I appreciate that, but—"

"Again, really?" Sonny said in exasperation when she stepped off of the elevator.

"I was just telling her she needed to respect boundaries. Sonny, please, she came here to warn us."

"Can you not have a conversation with her when you're dressed?"

"Come inside, let me explain," Dax pleaded.

Hesitantly, Sonny followed them through the door, as Zola folded her arms across her chest.

"You can wipe that smug look off of your face, or I will wipe it off for you, bitch," Sonny said as she shoulder-checked the skinny model, and the three of them retreated into Dax's apartment.

CHAPTER 26

The organ music played as people piled into the cathedral. Beverly watched in the mirror as her bridesmaid pulled the corset strings a little tighter on her gown. Her friends were positively giddy as they sipped their mimosas and whispered about the promise of drunk wedding sex.

The music changed and indicated that the parents of the bride and the groom were walking down the aisle. Beverly peeked her head out of the bridal room and caught a glimpse of her mother-in-law kissing her soon-to-be husband. He knocked elbows with his best man, threw his head back, and laughed.

She could hear the sound of his laughter resonate all the way through the church. It should have been music to her ears. She was about to pledge herself forever and always to this man. His laughter and happiness should have warmed her soul. It should have been contagious, but instead, it grated on her nerves. She suddenly realized the sound coming out of her soon-to-be husband's mouth made her stomach turn.

How could she not have realized this sooner? Why was this deal breaker just now occurring to her?

"We will see you up there, Bev. You look beautiful."

"Thanks," she whispered and watched as, one by one, each of her bridesmaids filed out of the room to walk down the aisle—down the aisle of her wedding.

She broke out in a cold sweat, and suddenly it felt like a brick was on her chest. She couldn't breathe. The corset seemed to get tighter with each inhale. This was more than just pre-wedding jitters. This was her subconscious stopping her from making the biggest mistake of her life.

Oh, God, Parker had been right all along.

Parker.

Rough around the edges, imperfect, egocentric, complex Parker. Suddenly, everything was crystal clear.

She gathered her skirt and looked around for an escape route.

The music began to play, and everyone stood for Beverly's grand entrance. It should have been the moment every girl dreamed about. Long moments passed. The crowd stirred and started to murmur, as the questions passed amongst them.

Her maid of honor tiptoed back to the bridal room. She gasped when she wasn't greeted by a nervous bride with cold feet, but instead an empty room with an open window, curtains blowing in the breeze.

She stepped timidly in front of the congregation, scared to break the news.

"She's gone."

*****

Parker stared into his amber-colored drink and watched as the foam dissolved, one bubble at a time. In many ways, the minutes felt like agonizing hours, but on the other hand, he wished he had had more time. Instead, he had to endure the torturous knowledge that she was taking herself off the market, probably right at this very moment. He wouldn't have another chance. He would have to respect her wishes.

But, man, was she wrong. Why couldn't she see what he did? She was stubborn and wrong. Did he mention that she was wrong?

"You need another drink, pal?" the bartender asked him.

"If I needed another drink, I would ask you for one."

The bartender held his hands up in mock surrender. "My bad, you looked thirsty."

"Why such a grouchy mood?" a voice from behind his barstool asked.

The feminine sound was the most exquisite melody that had ever graced his ears. He was afraid to turn around for fear that she was just a mirage that his mind had conjured up to relieve his physical self of his misery before the grief swallowed him whole.

Holding onto one shred of dignity and a glimmer of hope, Parker turned around slowly. Beverly stood adorned in lacey white, looking like something out of a dream. His breath caught in his throat.

"What are you doing here?" he croaked.

She wrung her hands nervously and shrugged her shoulders. Tears filled her eyes, and, when she tried to speak, her voice shook, and her lips quivered with emotion. "You told me to take a chance."

Parker was off of his barstool in seconds and wrapped her up in his strong protective arms. "I'm afraid to ask, but does that mean you aren't married?"

She buried her face in his shoulder. "No, I couldn't go through with it. How could I?"

He tilted her face to meet his eyes. "What made you change your mind?"

His eyes searched hers with such intensity she felt like they were burning right through her.

"I couldn't marry one man when my heart belongs to another."

"I was hoping you would say that," he said gruffly before his mouth crushed down over hers.

When they finally pulled away, they were both breathless.

"How did you know where to find me?"

"Lucky guess. It's where we met. It's like you knew I was going to show up here."

He smiled a boyish grin. "Trust me, I didn't know, but I was praying for divine intervention. I hoped you would come to your senses and admit to yourself what I was feeling all along."

She traced the line of his jaw. "And what was that?"

"That I'm madly and deeply in love with you and have been since the moment I saw you."

She kissed him tenderly. "I was hoping you would say that. Because I love you too, and it may have taken me a little longer to realize it, but now it couldn't be more clear."

"Do you really mean that?"

"Yes," she said earnestly.

"Good. You're a vision in that dress, and it would be a shame for it to go to waste."

"Are you suggesting we get married?"

"What do you say?"

"I think you're crazy."

"Crazy in love with you," he said seriously.

"Then what are we waiting for? Let's do it."

"You've made me a very happy man. I can't wait to spend the rest of my life with you. Will you do me the honor of being my wife?"

She smiled through tear-filled lashes. "I was hoping you would say that. And yes, yes I will."

ଓଓ

"Cut. I think we got it. That's a wrap."

Lillian and Dax high fived and made their way to the cheering stagehands.

Sonny dabbed her eyes, and Dax said, "So what did you think? Please tell me those are happy tears."

Sonny sniffed. "It was perfect. You two really did an amazing job. It was really a beautiful ending to a beautiful story."

Dax leaned in close and whispered in her ear. "See? Some stories do have a happy ending. You just have to have faith."

"How sweet," Zola said sarcastically as she walked by.

Sonny rolled her eyes. "Must you ruin everything? She's always around. If you really wanted to be with me, you would tell your ex to take a hike."

"Bitch, you are the one who stole my boyfriend, if you remember correctly," Zola countered.

"Believe that if you want, but I was just doing the job that I was hired to do. Dax is the one who approached me. He was very persistent, despite my pleas to keep it professional, but, as it would seem, like most men, he wants to have his cake and eat it too. But you're all talk, aren't you, Dax? Smooth words, that's your specialty, right? Or is it for being a heartbreaker? I knew I should have been more careful with you and with my heart. How could I be so naïve to allow you to hurt me this way?" Hot fat tears rolled down her cheeks. "How can you just stand there and not say anything?"

"I care about you, but I care about Zola too. You can't ask me to choose. I just need time to figure out where my head's at."

"Who cares what your head says? What about your heart? What does it tell you?" She shook her head in desperation. "I'll tell you what. If you can make heads or tails and finally make a decision, maybe you'll let me know. I'll be at Helen's, the little dive bar by my house. I will wait for you, but if you don't show, I'll assume you've made your decision, and then I'm done waiting. I won't give you any more of my time. I've got to take care of me, but I'll give you tonight. And then I'm done."

She wiped her eyes, and, as she turned on her heel and walked away, she saw the flashes of the media cameras capture every moment.

CHAPTER 27

When Sonny entered her apartment, she was in a rush to change her clothes, but Hudson stopped her in her tracks.

"Sonny, are you okay?"

"Yeah, of course."

"I mean, you're really fine?"

"Yes, Hudson, why wouldn't I be?"

"You seem frazzled. You know you can tell me anything, right?"

"Yes, I know, but I'm kind of in a hurry."

"Any place in particular?" he asked.

"Just grabbing some drinks," she tried to say flippantly.

"Want some company? I don't have any plans."

"I'm really sorry, Hudson, but it's something I have to do on my own."

"Oh, I get it. You have a hot date?"

"Something like that," she whispered through clenched teeth.

ꟹꟹ

Sonny had been gone for hours, and Hudson had a weird feeling that she wasn't being completely honest with him. They hadn't had a lot of time to catch up recently because she had been so busy with Daxton Knight's schedule.

Hudson's instincts told him that she cared about the actor more than she let on, but that girl had too much pride or was trying to be too sensible to admit it. He just hoped that Dax would treat her kindly and not take advantage of her. His reputation for being a womanizer was something that was hard to ignore. Sonny was a smart girl, and, hopefully, she was using her head on this one.

The phone rang and cut through his thoughts.

"Hello?"

"Is Sonny Winslow available?"

"No, I'm sorry, she isn't. Can I take a message?"

"Well, you can tell her that Maggie Mayfield called, and she'll want to speak with me right away. I believe I have an offer that she can't refuse."

"Does this have to do with her book?" Hudson asked excitedly.

"Maybe," the agent said coyly. "Will you just tell her to give me a call?"

"Yes, yes. Of course."

"If she's with Dax, tell him Maggie said hello."

When Hudson hung up the phone, he knew he couldn't wait to tell Sonny. She would want this kind of news immediately. He dialed her number as he headed out the door.

"Hey, Sonny, it's Hudson. I've got great news. A woman named Maggie Mayfield called here looking for you. She sounded like an agent and hinted that she was interested in giving you a book deal. I'm headed to meet you at Helen's, and I'll give you the rest of the details."

He grabbed a jacket and was out the door.

∞

"I have to pee."

"Well, you have to hold it," Dax said, irritated.

"Dax, I'm not a child. Who knows how long we'll be waiting? I have to go."

"If you don't want to be treated like a child, quit acting like one. We won't know how long we'll be waiting so maybe you shouldn't guzzle down so many liquids."

"But I can't help that I'm thirsty, Dax," she whined. "This is boring. Aren't you bored?"

"Zola, do you ever stop complaining? You said you were on board, so be on board without being such a pain in my ass. Sonny's sticking her neck out there, and we have to be ready."

His pulse twitched in his temple as he gripped the steering wheel and stared out his windshield. It had started to sprinkle, and he flipped the wipers to clear off the glass, slurping a drink of his coffee that had cooled to a lukewarm temperature. He watched patrons file into the bar, some carrying umbrellas, which he silently cursed because they served to also inhibit his view.

"You love her, don't you?" Zola said quietly.

Dax hesitated. "Why do you say that?"

"Come on, Daxton. I'm not blind. Anyone with eyes can see the way you look at her. It's obvious to everyone, but Sonny. And she has feelings for you too, you know? She may have a guard up, but she does. She hasn't been tarnished by the industry yet. Dax, my advice is to try and make sure it stays that way. It hardens you and, before you know it, you can't even recognize yourself anymore. I wasn't always this way. Maybe it's too late for me to get back to the girl I once was, but it's not too late for you, Dax."

"Hey, now. I know that, deep down, you're a good person, Zola. Otherwise, I wouldn't have been attracted to you, to begin with. You just need to listen to your gut. It'll guide you back to where you want to go."

"Thanks, Daxton. I appreciate your kind words, and I'll be okay. My ego may be bruised, but who am I to stand in the way of true love? No one wants to be that girl."

Dax squeezed her hand. "Someday, Zola, you'll make a man very happy, and you'll be glad you held out for the real deal."

"I hope so." She looked out the front windshield. "Dax, look. Isn't that Sonny's roommate? What's he doing here?"

Dax squinted past the umbrellas blocking his view and gasped in surprise. "Well, I'll be damned. That's Hudson, all right. I would have never pegged him as the stalker type. Come on, let's go," Dax said as he rushed toward the bar to stop him.

ଓଓ

Sonny swirled her drink and watched the condensation accumulate on the outside of the cup. A small droplet slowly rolled down the side of the glass, gaining speed as it made its journey stopping briefly before dropping on her thumb. She then wiped the dampness on her pants leg.

Who were they kidding with this amateur plan? Did they really think the stalker would buy the argument between her and Zola and then come looking for Sonny, hoping to form an alliance in the we-hate-Daxton-Knight club. It was a little far-fetched, but he did try to recruit Zola, so it was worth a try. They had nothing better to go on. What was the worst that could happen? If it was a lost cause, then it was a few hours wasted out of her life and some embarrassing headlines in the tabloids.

Sonny wished they hadn't had to make a public spectacle out of themselves, but they all agreed that they needed to be sure that their guy thought they were at odds and that she would bait him and, hopefully, draw out his identity.

At first, her adrenaline had her on the edge of her seat, but as the minutes turned to hours, she became more convinced that their plan would not work. She decided it was about time she allowed herself to use the restroom. She had a miserably full bladder for fear that she would miss her chance to catch the man who had been terrorizing them. She wanted to look the person the eyes who was responsible for Baby Sully's early entrance into the world and tell him exactly what she thought about him.

She pushed the button on the hand dryer and checked her reflection in the mirror. She was staring at the image of a pistol being aimed at the back of her skull.

Sonny started to scream, but the man holding the gum placed a finger over her lips indicating silence.

"Hello, Sonny," he said as he pressed the barrel against her temple. "I've been waiting for you. I think it's about time that you and I had a little talk about the company you've been keeping."

"Nate," she pleaded. "You don't have to do this. It's

not too late. If you turn yourself in now, you won't be in much trouble. We can explain everything."

"Shut up," he snarled and pressed the gun hard against her back. The barrel was cold and threatening against her bare skin. He stood close enough to her to block the view of the weapon as he pushed her toward the back entrance. "You are coming with me."

"Nate, please. Let's just talk about this."

"Shhh." He twisted the gun against her ribs, and his breathing became heavy. "It looks like old lover boy ended up showing up for you after all," Nate said as he spotted Dax's car across the street.

He pushed Sonny toward it.

"Looks like we just missed him too, maybe fate is on my side. Get in," he demanded as she shoved her across the seat. "Don't try any funny business, or I'll blow the pretty little actor's head off on the spot when he comes out. I've got nothing left to lose," he said as he revved the engine and squealed the tires on the low riding sports car. "Besides, I'm banking on him caring enough about you to come looking for you. And when he does, I'll be ready."

ᏣᏣ

Dax grabbed Hudson's shirt collar and, when he turned around, slammed his fist against Hudson's cheek.

Hudson tried to block his face. "What the hell are you doing, man?"

"Why are you stalking Sonny and me?" Dax spat in his face.

"What?"

"Don't play dumb, you son of a bitch. I hit now and ask questions later. You better start talking."

A man cleaning the bar started to walk toward them, and Hudson motioned for him to stay back and that the situation was under control.

"Dax, I'm not stalking you or Sonny. She filled me in about the odd circumstance a while back, and we haven't been around each other enough for me to get an update on the situation. I swear," Hudson said persuasively.

"Then what are you doing here?"

"I came to tell Sonny the good news. An agent called about her book, said she needed to talk to her soon to discuss a deal that was too good to pass up. I knew that Sonny would want to know immediately so I decided to tell her, so she could get the details and celebrate. The agent said to tell you hello. I assumed you were with Sonny."

Dax loosened his hold on Hudson's shirt and relaxed his stance somewhat.

"Will you please tell me what's going on? Where's Sonny, and why were you going to pulverize my face?"

Dax looked around, realized he didn't see Sonny, and his stomach flip flopped anxiously. "Zola, go check the ladies' room." He flipped through his phone until he found a picture of her. "Bartender, do you remember seeing this woman?"

"Yes, she was just at the bar moments ago. That's her drink she left there."

Dax picked up the drink and smelled it. Apple juice. She had been smart enough to keep her wits about her.

"Dax, she isn't in the bathroom. I asked a worker who was on a smoke break. He said he saw her leaving with a man just a short time ago. He said they looked awfully chummy, all cuddly like a couple."

"Dammit." Dax punched the mahogany bar in front of him. "He has her, and we missed it while we were busy accusing the wrong guy." He whirled around. "Come on, maybe they haven't made it that far."

They slipped out the front door, and the trio looked around wildly.

"Will you please tell me? Who has Sonny? What are we looking for?"

"We devised a plan to draw out the stalker. He propositioned Zola to help with our demise, and when she declined, we decided it was worth a shot to set him up. We staged an argument between the three of us and made sure the press heard it loud and clear. Sonny said she would wait here, and I was supposed to meet her with my decision between her and Zola. We hoped that our guy would be intrigued enough to try to win her over to the dark side and help him live out some sort of sick hatred and revenge, but while we were busy storming you, he swooped in on his prey. I should have never let her do this. We have to find her," Dax said, his voice filled with misery and angst.

"Dax, I've got some more bad news."

"What, Zola?" he asked in agony.

"Someone took your car."

ꕥꕥ

"Eventually, lover boy will have to come back home. And when he does, we'll be here waiting for him."

Nate had an evil glint in his eye and, without having to look, he reached under the doormat and retrieved the hidden spare key to Dax's apartment. The knowledge that he had access to them whenever he wanted sent chills down her spine, but she knew she had to act fast, or she may not get another opportunity.

While Nate was bent over, Sonny hammered both fists down as hard as she could on the base of his skull causing him to teeter forward, and, when he did, she jerked her knee upward connecting with his nose. A crunch erupted, and a string of curse words followed. She saw the first couple of drops of blood splat against the linoleum, but she didn't stick around to see the damage.

Sonny turned and ran quickly, debating whether to take the stairs or the elevator. It just so happened that the elevator was on their floor and the doors were open. She darted in and repeatedly pushed the button to close herself in.

"Come on, dammit, what is taking so long? Close already." Her voice sounded foreign to her own ears as she barely heard the shrill panic over the sound of her beating heart.

"Get back here, you bitch. I think you broke my nose," he grunted.

She could hear the sound of heavy footsteps approaching and then the doors decided to close. She exhaled and tried to think of her next plan.

All of a sudden the doors paused, and she looked down to see the steal toe of a boot and then the doors were propelled back open.

Nate stood in front of her blocking any chance at an exit, and she was covered with his own blood. His nose was still leaking like a faucet, and he wiped it away idly with the back of his hand.

"Thought you could outsmart me at my own game? I tried to do this the easy way, but I should have known you would prefer the hard way."

He reached into his pocket and drew out a syringe.

"What are you going to do with that?" she asked nervously.

"I'm going to make you more cooperative."

"Pharmaceutical sales. I guess you have access to a lot of different drugs."

She needed to keep him talking. Dax and Zola would know she was kidnapped by now. Help had to be coming. She had to avoid that needle by all costs.

He grunted. “Pharmaceutical sales. More like back alley drug deal.”

“Is there anything that you didn’t lie about?”

“I didn’t lie about being a baseball fan.”

She shook her head sadly. “Why are you doing this?”

“Because life isn’t fair, and it’s time to even the score.”

He lunged forward, and Sonny screamed. She was backed into a corner with nowhere to go, and she looked for an exit strategy frantically.

“Please don’t do this,” she begged and hated herself for it, but she was running out of options.

“Please don’t do this,” he mimicked in a tone dripping with sarcasm.

He pinned her against the back of the elevator with his forearm. She wiggled underneath his grasp, but he held her forcefully choking her underneath his weight.

She tried to pry his arm away from her throat and wrestle her way out from under him. She kicked and screamed, but it was to no avail as he plunged the needle into the side of her neck. A warm tingling sensation spread throughout her body, and she felt paralyzed.

“To answer your question. What’s my problem with Dax? Let’s see, where do I begin? For starters, he was a crappy brother.”

Shock registered on her face right before she went limp.

ଓଃଓଃ

"Nine-one-one, what is your emergency?"

"I need to report a kidnapping. A woman, Sonny Winslow, could be in danger."

"Okay slow down, sir. How long has Ms. Winslow been missing?"

"She was taken within the last thirty minutes, from Helen's on Fourth. I was supposed to be watching her, but she was seen leaving with an unknown man."

"So she was seen leaving a bar with a man?"

"Yes, but he's dangerous."

"Who's the man who took her?"

"I'm not sure."

"So how do you know he's dangerous?"

"Because I just know. Can we hurry this up? We need to find her, and I'll answer questions later."

"Sir, I'm just trying to make sure that Ms. Winslow wants to be found."

"She does, trust me. I'm not sure of the man's identity, but we have had problems with a stalker."

"Have you made a police report of the stalking."

"No, we were warned by our stalker not to. I'm realizing now just how idiotic we were to abide by his rules, but I'm reporting it now. I just hope that it's not too late."

"Okay, sir can I get your name?"

"Daxton Knight."

"The actor?"

"Yes."

"Do you have any idea where this person could have taken her?"

"We have already checked her place, and they aren't there. We're headed to my place next. Please send help now," he said, giving his address.

"Sir, we will dispatch officers to your house."

"Thank you. Tell them to hurry. Oh, and I believe he took my car."

When Dax clicked off the phone, Hudson squealed into the parking garage. Dax was out of the car before Hudson put the vehicle in park.

"My car's here. They're here," he yelled as he ran to the stairs, taking them two at a time. "Wait here for the police." Dax said a prayer under his breath as he jogged all the way to the top floor. "She has to be okay. She will be okay."

CHAPTER 28

Dax tried the front door to his apartment only to find it locked, his key not working. He pounded on the door. "Sonny, are you in there? Are you okay?" He pressed his ear against the wood and listened closely for any signs of Sonny. Nothing but silence came through from the other side of the wall. He punched the door harder. "I know you're in there, and I know that you took her, you son of a bitch. You've been watching our every move without revealing yourself. So quit being a coward. Show yourself." Dax waited a moment, and when he wasn't granted a response, he hammered the door with his fists in frenzied hysteria and screamed in desperation, "Show yourself, you coward."

His voice was raw with emotion and cracked as he strained against his vocal chords. "I said show yourself."

The last decibel he held out long and with emphasis to show his seriousness.

He was so angry, he could hardly see straight, his breathing was ragged, coming in harsh, shallow waves. He felt a change in the air behind him.

"Your wish is my command, little brother."

Dax's spine went rigid right before his stalker grabbed the back of his head and slammed it against the wall. Everything went black.

"Let the games begin," the wicked voice whispered as he dragged him across the threshold.

ᘓᘓ

Dax felt groggy, disoriented, and when his eyelids fluttered open, pain seared through his temples, and the reality came flooding back to him.

He recognized the floor he was laying on as his own and knew that he must have only been out for a couple of minutes. He looked around, anxiously checking for Sonny, without letting his perpetrator know that he was awake.

He saw two female legs laying a short distance away. The rest of her body was blocked by the sectional sofa that took up a good portion of the living room. He'd recognize those shapely stems anywhere. They belonged to Sonny and were sickly still. His whole body went cold, and he felt as though he was going to jump out of his skin as the fear quickly overtook him.

"I know you're awake. You can quit pretending to be knocked out. Besides, we may not have much time, so we need to get this party started. It really is a pity. I've been looking forward to this moment for a long time, and it's is a shame that now that it's here, I'm being rushed. But that's the way of the world. We don't always get what we want unless your name is Daxton Knight, then you always get your way. Right, Dax?"

Dax looked up and made eye contact with Mike, his stepbrother. He looked at him for the first time in years. For a moment, he was still surprised, as if until he saw the man with his own eyes, that it was just too far-fetched to be true.

"Is she..." Dax looked over at Sonny but was too fearful of the answer to finish the question.

"Dead? No, not yet. If I killed her before you got here, where would the fun be in that? The whole point is to torture you."

"What did you do to her? If you hurt her, I swear I'll kill you myself."

"Oh, Daxton Knight, the super star wants to be a super hero." Mike laughed out loud. "I'm sorry that's not the way this script is written as I'm in charge now, and I say how it ends. This time I come out on top."

"Is that what this is? Jealousy. You're mad that I'm more successful than you?" Dax asked Mike as he made his way toward Sonny. "Come on, baby. Open your eyes. Come on, Sonny. Are you okay? Sweetheart, open those beautiful eyes."

Sonny groaned.

"That's it. That's a girl. Come back to me, baby. What did you give her?" Dax asked angrily.

"Oh, relax. She'll wake up soon enough. It's just a little concoction to make her more cooperative." Mike squeezed the bridge of his nose and pain filtered across his face. "I've got to tell you, your girl, she's a feisty one. That must be fun for you."

He wiggled his eyebrows at Dax suggestively, and it made Dax's stomach turn in disgust.

In another world, it was completely normal for two brothers to disclose intimate details of their bedroom escapades with each other, but it was not okay for this man to even speak Sonny's name.

Rage filled Dax, and he sprang up like a panther ready to pound on his prey. He almost had his hands around Mike's neck when Mike pulled the gun on him and shoved it underneath Dax's chin. He cocked it with a solemn click.

"You don't want to do that. I'm locked and loaded. One pull of the trigger, and I can blow that pretty little face of yours clean off."

Dax tried to swallow, but the hard metal of the gun was pressed against his Adam's apple. "What do you want from me?"

"I want payback. Payback for taking away my father, payback for making sure the attention was always on you. You took everything from me, always got the lucky break. Your whore of a mother broke up my family. It destroyed my mom. She was never the same after that, and she was too depressed to care for her own son. And it's not like it was any better when I was with my father. He was too busy being focused on his new slut of a wife and her shining star of a son. You were a brat, but people took to you for some reason, and I was ignored, overlooked. I was living in the shadows, replaced by you. My father never had a drinking problem until your mom came along. And now he'll forever be haunted by the reputation that he killed her in the accident. Sure, physically he was there, but mentally he was gone. Checked out. We were on our own after that. We should have been brothers, but we weren't, man. As soon as you could, you hightailed it out of there without so much as asking how I was going to be. Then you went on to bask in your millions, flaunting it all over television and magazines with no mention of me at all. Did you ever wonder about me? Or did you just forget?"

"Mike." Dax shook his head. "I had no idea you felt this way, and I didn't know you ever wanted a relationship with me."

"You never asked."

"For that, I'm sorry."

"Too little, too late. I'll make sure you never forget again."

"It's not too late, Mike. We can talk about this. Maybe we can have a relationship in the future."

Mike shook his head. "No, I don't think so. It's too late for that. You were too busy spending your fortune, walking around with the flavor of the week to think about me. I was left struggling to make ends meet. When we lost our house, my wife left me. I had nothing, and it wasn't fair. What did you do to deserve all of the lucky breaks while I was left in the hell hole to rot?"

"Mike, I'm sorry to hear about your wife."

"I bet you didn't even know I was married, did you."

"No, I didn't. I'm sorry about your childhood and the rough breaks, but you can't go around hurting innocent people and taking your anger for me out on other people. You hurt an innocent baby."

Mike shuffled his feet and repositioned his hand around the gun. "I don't want to talk about that. I warned Sonny to stay away from you, and she didn't heed my warning. I thought about all the ways that I could make her pay, but after I read her book, I knew that was the way to hit her where it hurt."

From somewhere close by they could hear sirens and, from the sounds of it, they were getting closer.

Dax could see the sweat pop out on Mike's face as he nervously looked over at Sonny's limp body. Dax needed to keep Mike as calm as possible if he wanted to get them both out of there alive. Mike wiped the damp perspiration on his jeans as he switched the gun from one hand to another. His movements were jerky, and he began to pace.

"What did you do? Are the police coming here? You called them, didn't you? Why would you do that?"

"Is it that so inconceivable to you? I've had a stalker who was getting more unpredictable by the day, who then kidnapped my girlfriend and drugged her. I thought you were going to kill us. Why wouldn't I call the police?"

"You said you thought I was going to kill you. What makes you so sure I'm not?"

Mike lifted the gun and aimed it at Dax. "Should I start with you or your girlfriend?" He looked over at where Sonny was laying. "Wait, where did she go?" he asked, panicked.

Dax looked in the same direction and saw that Sonny was no longer in her previous spot.

"That bitch!" Mike roared.

Just then, Sonny dove out from the kitchenette and stabbed a fork in the side of Mike's neck. She let out a warrior scream as she plunged it deeper. Mike's eyes bulged in surprise. Dax knocked the gun out of his hand and scrambled to pick it up. He fumbled to secure it.

"Who are you calling a bitch?" Sonny said, running toward Dax.

"Are you okay?" Dax asked as he grabbed her face, looking her over.

"I'm okay."

They returned their attention back to their attacker when they heard him gasp and fall to his knees. He clutched at the fork in the side of his neck. "How could you do this to me? You're my brother."

"But you were never mine." Dax approached him and grabbed his chin, looking him directly in the eye. "If you were, you wouldn't have hurt the people closest to me. I have no respect for you, but I'm still not going to let you die."

He said it as he applied pressure to Mike's neck to slow the bleeding. Just then the door swung open.

"Police, drop the weapon," the swat team screamed as they swarmed the room.

CHAPTER 29

Dax looked through the windows of the bookstore. It had been months since he had seen her last. She was even more beautiful than he remembered. Being away from her had only made him want her more.

He watched her smile and interact with her fans, and his heart swelled with pride.

"Are you going to stand out here all day or are you going to be a man and go say hello to her?"

Dax smiled when he heard the voice behind him.

"Ms. Maggie Mayfield, my favorite agent," he said affectionately.

"Mr. Knight, one of my favorite clients."

"Ouch, that hurts."

"Oh, hush. You know I'll always have a special place for you, but I have to say I'm so glad I tried my hand as a literary agent. They love her. Her books are flying off the shelves, and we already have a three-book contract with a major publishing company. Before you know it, we'll be talking movie rights. I'm so glad that you sent me her manuscript. You were right about her. She's something special."

"Yes. Yes, she is," he mused.

Maggie smiled a knowing smile.

"Why are you looking at me like that?"

"Because I know you better than you think. Now go in there and talk to her."

"Thanks, Maggie."

Dax took a deep breath and made his way into the bookstore. When she saw him, she stopped mid conversation, surprise etched on her pretty features.

She signed the woman's book and excused herself gracefully. She lowered her lashes as she walked toward him. "Hey, what are you doing here? I thought you were busy promoting *For Better or Worse.*"

"And miss the big event from the hottest new author. I wouldn't dream of it."

She smiled. "You're so full of it, but in all seriousness, thank you for putting my book in the right hands. It means a lot. I couldn't have done it without you."

"Yes, you could," he corrected her. "I've always known you were something special. I'm so proud of you. You're going to make it in the big time, but the best part—" He hesitated and brushed a piece of hair away from her face. "You're so grounded and kind, it won't change you in the slightest."

Sonny's face grew serious. "Do you mean that?"

"Are you joking? You're one of the best people I have ever known. You're a rare one, a diamond in the rough."

"Don't feed me a line, Dax. You haven't spoken to me since that night. The movie was finished, the stalker turned out to be your stepbrother, case closed. You left without even a goodbye. I stabbed a man in the neck who barely survived, and still, not even worthy of a phone call?"

"Sonny, please don't get upset on your big day. The last sight I saw before being questioned by the police was you being rolled away on a stretcher while being administered oxygen. That was my fault, and you and I both know it could have ended much differently. I'm sorry if you felt I abandoned you or if I hurt you, but I figured the best thing I could do was stay away."

"How do you know what's best for me? You can't even figure out what it is that you want."

"I know what I want, Sonny," he whispered. "I've known from the very beginning when I stepped off that plane. I want—no, let me clarify—I need you. I guess I just thought I was being admirable by staying away."

"Well, quit thinking so much, would you?"

A grin spread across his face. "So does this mean you forgive me?"

"I didn't say all that. I just didn't want to waste one of my books with a personalized message that you requested."

"You personalized my copy?" His face lit up with satisfaction. "Well, let me read it."

"Kiss me first, Daxton Knight."

Dax did not hesitate. His mouth captured hers and any reservations of self-doubt and guilt went away. He was right where he needed to be.

"Kissing you is like coming home," he said gruffly. "Sonny, I love you, and I think I have from the moment I met you."

Tears pooled in her eyes, and a smile played on the corner of her lips. "Oh, thank goodness, you said it first. It would have been rather embarrassing if you had read it on the inside cover of your book and didn't feel the same."

"Well, well. Is that what you inscribed to me?"

"Yes, it is. I'm sure you hear it all the time from adoring fans, but I do love you with all my heart, even if at times it has been against my will."

"If it helps, I've never heard it before and had it mean anything."

"And now?" she asked.

"It means everything."

About the Author

Jen Midkiff, also known as JD Davis, is from a mid-western town where she works as a hairstylist. She is a devoted wife and mother to triplet toddler boys. When she isn't running half marathons, managing her salon, or taking care of her family, she enjoys writing in her spare time. While *Judicial Justice* was her first published debut as an author, she has more mystery romance novels that will be coming out in the future. Be on the lookout for her upcoming titles.